THE GOD
OF
NIGHTMARES

PAULA FOX

NORTH POINT PRESS

San Francisco   1990

LIBRARY OF CONGRESS
CATALOGING-IN-PUBLICATION DATA
Fox, Paula.
The god of nightmares / Paula Fox.
p.   cm.
ISBN 0-86547-432-X
I. Title.
PS3556.094G6   1990
813'.54—dc20   89-37112

Fic

For Ellen Adler
and
In Memory of Leopold de Sola

    I have a feeling that my boat
has struck, down there in the depths,
against a great thing.
                            And nothing
happens! Nothing . . . Silence . . . Waves . . .

—Nothing happens? Or has everything happened,
and are we standing now, quietly, in the new life?

                             Juan Ramón Jiménez

THE GOD
OF
NIGHTMARES

Part One

Part One

CHAPTER

ONE

In the early spring of 1941, thirteen years after he'd left home, my father, Lincoln Bynum, died far away from my mother and me in a seaside village in northern California. My mother's astonishment at this news was so great, I realized for the first time that she'd believed all those years that in the long run he'd return.

Actually, he had been dead for nearly a month when a pencil-written note addressed to me came from the woman he had been living with.

"He didn't suffer," she wrote. "He was happy and suntanned and hopeful. But his poor dear heart gave out. It was all of a sudden right after we'd had our breakfast. I'm sorry I couldn't write before. I've been sick. I had to clean out the cabin and move. He didn't leave any keepsakes or I would send them to you. He often spoke about you."

1928

It was signed *Bernice*. No last name.

"We might never have known!" my mother cried out, the note falling from her hand as she dropped to her knees in front of a glass cabinet that held the trophies—cups, faded ribbons, statuettes—my father's horses had won for him. "I would have gone on . . ." she moaned.

She could only have meant she would have gone on deluding herself. She covered her face with her hands. I picked up the envelope. It bore no return address and the stamp was upside down. Our address was so faint as to be barely legible. *New York* was written as one word, as if at the last, Bernice had been unable to muster the strength to lift the pencil from the paper. The envelope suggested disaster more than my mother kneeling on the floor, weeping. It intimated a grief that was not hallucinatory but natural.

"Why did she write to *you*!" my mother suddenly shrieked.

For a moment I was stunned as though she'd slapped me. Did she imagine I'd been in secret communication with the woman all along? I couldn't think. Her woeful face, her eyes starting from her head, the squashed wet circle of her open mouth seemed vile, stupid.

I turned my back to her and although I answered in a whisper, "I guess she would have been mortified to write to you," she heard me.

"Mortified?" she questioned bitterly. "A woman like that!"

"A woman like what?" I asked.

She didn't answer my question but mimicked a phrase from the note in a falsetto voice, " 'his poor dear heart.' "

"For God's sake, get up, Mother," I ordered her. "His heart

stopped. For all the good he's done us, he might have died thirteen years ago!"

We had spoken about him less and less as the years passed. He was like a song I had known long ago that had faded away, first the words, then the melody, until only the title remained, *Father*. I began to cry, but whether it was from sorrow or its absence, I couldn't tell.

I heard the creak of a floorboard, a groan, the rustle of cloth as my mother stood up. I heard her footsteps, then felt her arms around me, her small cold ear against my neck.

"Hush . . . hush . . ." she murmured. "We'll be all right. Haven't we always been all right? You'll see."

Soon, my mother would resolve to become cheerful. This last year I had begun to wonder if it was possible to have courage, or at least to be stoical, in the face of life's afflictions without at the same time betraying reality. Although I'd been shocked by the revelation of my mother's faith in my father's eventual return, and her dismay that it was not to be, the plain emotion of it stirred me.

Soon after my father's departure, I had ceased to confide my feelings to her. I had an almost physical dread—as though it would make me ill—of her telling me to look on the bright side of things, to believe that everything works out in the end, to remember that every dog has its day, this last avowed with slightly more spirit than the other sayings she had ready for what she called the rainy days of life.

One twilight, only a moment after she had mentioned just such a triumphant dog (this, in response to my laconic report

to her of why I lost my summer job: the niece of the dry-goods
store owner, for whom I had been working as a clerk, turned up
unexpectedly and needed the work more than I did, the owner
said when he fired me) a real dog, its condition pitiful, limped
into sight along the road that ran in front of our house. I called
to my mother, who was sitting on the sofa mending a torn pillowcase, and told her I wanted to rescue the poor creature. She
came to my side and looked through the window over which I
had been about to draw the shade, as was our custom at that
hour of the day.

"The animal is perfectly all right," she said. "It's just going
home." She gripped my wrist and recited a few lines from "El-
egy Written in a Country Churchyard."

"It's not a 'lowing herd,'" I interrupted her. "It's a starving
dog."

"What an old gloomy gus you are!" she observed tranquilly
and went back to the sofa and her mending. I could no longer
see the animal. I began to consider the trouble it would have
caused if I had brought it into the house, the diseases it might
have. I remember the lethargy that then came over me like a
swoon, and the certainty as I stood there, my hands like lead
weights at my sides, that it had partly been my mother's importunate and bullying optimism and the hardened heart which
was its consequence that had abandoned my father to his misery, left him alone with it, and finally driven him away from us.

I recollected that moment and those thoughts now as I
watched her slowly stir the soup she was warming for our supper.

"Soup will do, won't it, Helen?" she asked. "It's too sorrow-
ful a day for cooking."

The faint but steady clink of the spoon against the side of the pot suggested a dejected signal of distress. In the oilcloth thumbtacked to the kitchen table, at the side where I always sat, I saw a large hole, my doing, worked at over the years with finger or spoon. She half turned to gaze at me, still stirring. "This, too, shall pass," she said.

We had not seen my father since he had left a few weeks after my tenth birthday. He rarely wrote—a few times a year. Once he sent a money order for fifty dollars. Once he mentioned that he had met a kindly widow, Bernice. I might have forgotten his face if it had not been for the photographs that stood on nearly every table in our house. There were horses with him in all save two: a large sepia-toned wedding picture, and one of him holding me in his arms, an infant in a long white gown. Horses had been his passion. He had ruined himself because of them.

From my bedroom at the back of the house, I could see the empty stable, the paddock, a small hay barn, two tumbledown sheds, a quarter-mile course, and beyond its furthest boundary, a meadow and a forest of red pine. When I looked down at the oblong of the stable, the course, the foremost rank of pine rising like a cliff face, I imagined I was moving around in my father's mind just as, when a child, I moved through the stable, the barn, around the weathered planks of the course fencing, at the base of whose posts still grew clumps of Queen Anne's lace. I had gathered bouquets of it, filling up as many jam jars as my mother would spare me while he and a stableboy tended the horses.

It's true I had nearly forgotten his features—even though the photographs showed me the elements of a face, his face— but not his presence. All I had to do to conjure it up was to go to the stable and breathe in the enduring smell of horses, of worn leather, of grain whose dry, throat-tickling field smell still lingered in barrels where it had once been stored and from which still issued in flight now and then a gauzy minute insect, the descendant of generations, a kind of animate dust.

He had put me on a chestnut mare, Felicity, when I was three. The great beast was like a landscape to me. When I watched my father gallop the course on a two-year-old he had high hopes for, it was as though he was riding the earth. After he left, my mother told me to stay away from the stable; one of those "horse things" might fall on me, she said. But I went nearly every day after school.

In the tack room dust motes rained through rays of sunlight and settled ever more thickly on bridles and bits, nosebands and curb reins, on shelves of currying brushes, rusted stirrups, dirt-caked work gloves, pails, empty liniment jars, shovels for mucking, all the "horse things" my mother had warned might fall on me. I knew they wouldn't. Though I moved carelessly among them and sometimes handled them, they were only relics, and like my father, in the past.

Mustard-colored blankets and saddlecloths moldered in heaps on the floor. His best English saddle straddled a horizontal post, the leather bearing the imprints of where his knees had pressed, the stirrups raised to the length of his bent legs.

No matter how cold the brief afternoons of deep winter were, I went to the stable and stood on tiptoe to peer into the dark stalls, reciting to myself what names of horses I could remember. I walked down a ramp constructed of great fieldstones that led outdoors, recalling how the thumping sound of the horses' hooves would change, when they emerged from the brown and grain-dusty shadows of the stable, to a sharp, ringing, celebratory clip-clop. Alongside the ramp stood an old green-painted horse carrier, its tusklike shafts rammed into the ground. I would climb into it, breathing in the smell of horses so strongly concentrated in its narrow space, a kind of horse broth that I drank in until I grew dizzy.

Of all the foolish things my mother said, none was more foolish than her ordering me not to go to the stable. Yet I think she knew I went there, she must have known, but I was a child and didn't know she could see through walls and into my deepest inclinations.

She said my father had lost a fortune, and that if he'd been a less impulsive man, he could have salvaged something from the run of awful luck that began with a mare's false pregnancy. "He didn't do a blessed thing right, after then," she said. "He simply didn't know how to grin and bear it as we all must." By the time she spoke those words, I had begun to believe grinning was a way of not bearing it.

He raised his stud fees exorbitantly because he had what he judged to be the stallion of the century. "He was tantalized— he thought that horse had flash, greatness. Being tantalized can drive a person crazy." He had been wrong about the stallion, wrong about a two-year-old who couldn't make it out of the starting gate in his first race. He began to quarrel with all the veterinarians within a hundred miles of where we lived, just northeast of Poughkeepsie. Though my mother affected not to know a thing about horse gear, she didn't conceal her knowledge about racehorses and their care and what disasters could occur if they were over- or undertrained. My father had gone to both extremes with his most promising ponies.

"He knew better, so he must have helped the bad luck along," I once said to her. I was sixteen. The only thing I was sure of was that anything an adult did was an act of conscious will, perverse and stupid though it might be. At my words, she returned to the table the wedding picture she had been holding and staring at.

"Why would he have done that?" she asked indignantly. "He didn't adore being poor, after all. No. It was that mare. He got so low in his mind, his judgment was no good. He was confused, Helen. He panicked. I tried to make him see all the good things we still had. Oh! If you only knew how I tried!"

I did know. I had heard her speak to him at supper time as she spoke to me whenever she thought I was downcast.

"Keep your sense of perspective," she would say. "Think of those poor people who went through that earthquake out west a few years ago and lost their homes and everything they owned. Think of the Armenians, massacred or starving to death. Look right this instant at that lovely potato on your plate, Helen. Look at it, little girl! It's all yours! So pack up your troubles in your old kit bag . . ." And with a conspiratorial smile, as though we'd routed a petty-minded, grudging, horribly selfish third person at the table, she would begin to speak of other matters.

I used to wonder what she imagined Armenians, restored to life and well-fed, would concern themselves with if not daily life and its troubles, those human concerns that from the huge perspective of catastrophe dwindled down to nothing. "The world is going to end in a few million years," I once shouted at her, "so why did we bother with a new furnace?"

"Don't be sarcastic," she remonstrated. "Sarcasm is not attractive in a girl."

She never asked me why I was downcast when I made an effort to make her notice me by sitting morosely in a corner for an hour or sighing loudly and often. But there were times when I could not help telling her what was bothering me. Either way, she said the same things.

During the conversation about my father's bad luck, she asked me, "Don't you recall how grumpy your father became?"

"Grumpy!" I repeated, scornful of the childish, homely word —a word like the thunk of a beanbag. Yet I had recognized a pleading note in her voice, as though she were trying to persuade me of a thing she didn't entirely believe herself.

In memory, I saw my father, so thin I could see the knobby shape of his ribs through his shirt, leaning against a stable wall, staring out at the course as I slowly drew down from around his neck a faded ascot, trying to get his attention.

Well—he left, and my mother, with a competence I could not but admire, made a plan and carried it through and kept us going.

Her widowed father gave her a sum of money, telling her it was her inheritance, and she was not to expect anything more when he died. I suspect Grandfather George was glad to give it to her, relieved not to have to think much about her or her sister, my Aunt Lulu, in his latter years.

Such was his aloofness, an air he had of being without any

earthly ties, that it was hard for me to imagine what he felt about being the father of two showgirls. My mother had told me, proudly, that he had studied philosophy at the University of Heidelberg. Perhaps his readings there gave him the stoicism, later on when he came home to the United States, to endure his job as the manager of a small pharmaceutical company that made opium-laced cough medicines. For a brief time, I was interested in him. I had read a novel in which students at German universities were perpetually engaged in duels that left ravishing scars on their faces, fascinating to scores of beautiful women. His given name was Luther; his face was without scars, and on the rare occasions I saw him, he had to be reminded by my mother what my name was.

She had six cabins, each with a tiny kitchen, built by a local carpenter. During the summer and fall, people stayed in the cabins for as long as two weeks. Now and then a motorist would stop for the night. We made over two of our four bedrooms for such transients, and after she had moved to her bedroom a Chinese lacquered chest that my father had given her as a wedding present, she turned the living room into an office and reception room. The dining room remained untouched, my father's turf magazines in orderly stacks and his account ledgers on a table near the vitrine that held his prizes.

For eleven years my mother had managed the cabin business with a steady hand, calling it our little ship that had come through the storm. "The Good Ship Lollypop," I called it to myself.

We were often on the verge of sinking, at the beginning of the venture. As I grew older, I was able to help her more, especially after I graduated from high school. There was no possibility of my going on to college, but I felt no burning desire to go. The passage of money from the hands of the *guests*, as Mother called the people who rented the cabins, to an old metal toolbox she kept on the floor of her bedroom closet and from which bills were paid out for repairs on the property and our Ford, our shoes and food and electricity, the dentist and the doctor, made it clear to me that what we had in hand was all we had.

On errands into Poughkeepsie, I drove past Vassar College. I halted the car once, my attention caught by a perfect picture of a girl about my age. She was leaning against a tree, her eyes closed, a pile of books near her feet. She was wearing a plaid skirt, a green sweater and scuffed saddle shoes, and her auburn hair glowed in the sunlight like the healthy pelt of an animal. The college, that girl a few yards away from where I was sitting in the idling car, seemed as remote as a French chateau, its owner posed at its great doors dressed in a huge-skirted ballgown, in a photograph I had seen in a magazine a guest had left in one of the cabin toilets.

I couldn't quite believe my father had actually once had a fortune. There was no evidence of it in our old but undistinguished house. Maybe part of it had been the forest of red pine we had sold two years after he'd gone. He'd left my mother the deed to the property and $311 in cash, all that was left from the sale of the last of his horses.

My grandfather died shortly after the cabins were erected, and he was true to his word. There was no further inheritance. When there was a financial crisis, such as happened one bitter

January when we had to buy an oil burner to replace the coal
furnace—an ailing capricious beast that lived in the cellar, and
which we had tended for many years, banking it at night hoping
the embers would last so we would not have to rise, crimped
with cold, in the pale frozen dawn to start it up—my mother
would have to borrow money or sell off one of the few trinkets
she had saved from the time when she was one of Florenz Ziegfeld's glorious girls.

During the first year of my father's absence, we didn't know
where he was. Then he settled into the same California seaside
village where he died. He wrote us a note with two sentences,
giving his address and expressing the hope that we were getting
along all right.

"Did he hate us?" I asked her.

An expression of horror crossed her face. She uttered a
sound, low, harsh. It was like a growl. Her right hand rose as
though to strike me. Instead she threw her arms around me.
"My God!" she exclaimed over and over. When she released
me, she said in her normal, rather high, sweet voice, "He loves
us. He will always love us."

I did not seriously believe he hated us, but I didn't believe
what she said either. It was something else. He had thrown us
off like a burden he had found intolerable, beyond his capacity
to bear.

Once she had his address, my mother wrote him regularly,
long letters I never read which, she assured me with a somewhat saintly smile, were largely about me. I think I was ame-
nable enough as a rule, but I could not do as she always asked
me to and write to him myself or even add a postscript to her

letters. A wordless edginess would take hold of me when I saw her sitting at the dining table, staring at the turf magazines, sheets of writing paper in front of her, his old fountain pen in her hand.

I was engulfed by emotion. I sweated with it. The thought of writing "Hello, Daddy" to that unanswering existence out there in California made me want to run wildly out the door and down the newly widened road that went past our house toward the Berkshires.

She wouldn't ask him for help. Apart from one money order, he sent nothing. "I'm sure he needs every penny he's got," she said to me the morning the coal furnace gave out. "Your father only knew about horses—he wasn't cut out for the life of a wage earner."

I felt a flash of rage. For an instant my vision blurred and there was a bitter taste in my mouth. "Why doesn't he have to do what other people do?"

She stared at me in shocked surprise. Her mouth worked silently for a moment. Then, speaking in a hushed voice as though I'd gone mad and she must calm me, she said, "But that's the way he is. And we must put a good face on it."

It was her credo. I detested it. It was like an order to fool yourself. Yet I suppose the sense that she had some choice in how she behaved helped her through the hard times when she felt overwhelmed by the necessity of providing for the two of us, the bewilderment my father's desertion had caused her, her unavailing aloneness.

The question of a divorce never arose. I think she would have fought it as she would have fought for her life—or mine.

He rarely wrote. The last letter she got from him came a few days before my twenty-first birthday and concerned it. She read a few of its unadorned sentences to me, her voice rising in consternation. My father wrote that she described me as a child even though I was about to attain my majority. He wondered if in some fashion she was preventing me from leaving home and living a life of my own. By the time she put the single sheet of paper down on the kitchen table, she looked stricken.

"How *could* he think I'd keep you here against your wish?" she asked sadly.

My first impulse was to defend him. But as I glimpsed his small, neat handwriting on the page, as legible as print, when I considered that he had never once written to me directly, I was ashamed of my impulse. It was preposterous. What did anything he'd written have to do with me? That he wrote at all was because of my mother's insistence, her unending struggle to keep their connection living. It also occurred to me that his brief notes to her were simply a kind of impersonal courtesy. I remembered his unfailing good manners even with the often brutal rich people who had come to inspect his horses.

The last sentence of the letter—which she had not noticed on first reading because she was so distressed by what he'd written about me—changed her mood dramatically. He asked her to send him a photograph of herself in one of her Follies costumes. "Oh dear!" she cried. "I think the only one I have left is a group picture. Imagine his wanting one!"

As though the meaning of my father's words could touch me only when her attention was no longer on them, I felt a powerful desire to be elsewhere. In a nameless city, I imagined my hand reaching for a cord to turn on a light in a place entirely my own. But what would I do? And could she run the cabins without me?

"Do you think he actually wants to show a picture of me to that woman?" she asked. She was rummaging through a box of photographs she kept on the bottom shelf of a small bookcase. She chose one at last, gazing at it for a moment before she held it out for me to see. It was of a group of chorus girls barely covered by scraps of beaded white cloth, each girl holding up a huge plumed fan. She pointed at one, a little shorter than the other girls, flaunting her plume valiantly, her mouth painted in a smiling cupid's bow.

"You," I said.

"Me," she said in a hushed voice.

In her question about what my father intended to do with the photograph, I thought I had heard a touch of spite, even of triumph. I could hardly believe it, but I wanted to.

I was most aware of the passage of time when the cold weather began, more so than on my birthdays, even my twenty-first.

The hills among which we lived seemed to narrow, to close us into the green bloom of summer. The sun rose, the moon waxed and waned, the valley held the world. But when the deciduous trees lost their leaves and the meadows grew sere and tawny, I could see the roads leading out of the valley, and the Hudson River flowing south, and I would be discontented all day long.

The evening of the day we learned of my father's death, Mother said, "You really must leave, strike out for yourself.

Lulu and I did." Her tone was dry. The notion came to me that I had been a talisman who would ensure my father's ultimate return to her. My usefulness was, in a sense, over.

All traces of the soubrette she had been, the glorified girl who had exhibited herself for Florenz Ziegfeld and caught my father's attention, vanished that day. Until then, a suggestion of the flirtatious prettiness she had once had lingered about her despite her increasing weight, her stodgy, neglected clothes and the strain that showed on her face from years of living on the edge.

I had seen workmen startled as they glimpsed a passing wantonness in her face and stance. While she spoke to them in the placid, chatty middle-aged voice I had come to think of as somewhat of a pose—it was in so different a voice she spoke to me—they looked at her silently and answered her questions a little tardily, their lips slack and languorous.

She had aged so in the few hours since she read Bernice's note. Hope for my father's homecoming had kept her taut. She had lost her belief in the future. She had connived at a delusion; now life had gone hollow. His death was overshadowed by the more terrible truth that he had never intended to return. There was nothing now to put a good face on.

At the very moment she told me I must leave, I felt an avid desire to do so. She said it again. "Yes. You must go now."

She was staring at the old tablespoon with which she'd been stirring the soup. Its edge was worn away. "This is me," she said, holding it out for me to see. Then she dropped it in the sink.

"Everything here can nearly run itself. I'll get a girl from

Poughkeepsie to help me days. Your father was right. You should have left years ago. You'll be twenty-three in October. If you can't think of a reason to go, I'll give you one. You do want to go, don't you?"

She looked at me closely to read my face and, having read it, smiled. It was the sort of smile that comes to people's faces when some secret foretelling of theirs has come true. It was not amiable. "I see that you do," she observed, adding like an aside to herself, "There are feelings I have entirely forgotten."

"I haven't got a suitcase," I said.

She laughed aloud. "What nonsense!" she cried. "Well, then—we'll wrap up your little things in a kerchief, tie it to a stick, and off you'll go like Charlie Chaplin! Are you thinking of Matthew? I can tell you now that I always felt you were just passing the time where he's concerned. He's settled and stale. And he's nearly forty, too old by far!"

"I'm fond of him."

"Oh, fond! *Fond* is for dogs and cousins. *Fond* is for pale meager folk who don't want to be bothered! He hasn't a touch of your father's style."

"What style is that?" I asked coldly.

"Don't, don't . . . " she begged. Tears started in her eyes. "Where did she bury him?" she asked the kitchen ceiling with a sob. Her head and shoulders drooped. "You'd think that woman could have at least told us that. They do bury people in California, don't they? I could have taken flowers and sat beside his gravestone . . . if he has one. Oh, to think how diminished he was! They lived in a cabin! Did you notice that in her note? A cabin . . . "

"You've been crying for hours, Mother. It does no good."

"That's why I'm crying," she said. She wiped her eyes with her fists doubled as a child does. "They're all gone now. His whole family. Do you remember darling Uncle Morgan? Dead so long . . ."

"I remember him," I answered. Night had come. The kitchen window was a black square. She peered through it standing on tiptoe, her slender ankles rising out of the high-collared cloth slippers she had not taken off that day. She sniffed a little and came to sit at the kitchen table across from me. "I don't really want to live alone, not yet," she said, touching with one finger the carved wooden ring that circled her napkin, which was, like mine, frayed and stained. There would have to be a washing tomorrow. "And I have an idea." She looked up at me and was silent for a moment. She folded her hands and fingers into a little church, the two thumbs pointing up, the steeple.

"You go to New Orleans and see if you can get your Aunt Lulu to come up here and stay with me, for a while anyhow. There's nothing to be gained by my writing her. She doesn't answer letters no more than your father—" she hesitated, then brought out, "did."

I felt a rush of pity for her. Whether or not she had deluded herself all these years with a fairy tale about reuniting with my father, the tale had ended bitterly for her.

"I didn't know Aunt Lulu was in New Orleans," I said, choosing not to think of the momentousness of what she was saying. But as swiftly as a swallow flying past a window at dusk, a shadowed image of myself somewhere else came and went.

Lulu George had been a Ziegfeld girl, too. When the Follies closed down in 1931, she began an acting life. She joined a repertory company and became quite well known as an Ibsen actress. Then, according to my mother, she threw her career away for a man who wouldn't, in the long run, have her.

How did a woman do that? Throw her life away for a man? My mother grew vague when I pressed her for details. I concluded she didn't really know a thing about Lulu and might even have invented the whole affair. There had been a short-lived marriage. A small announcement of it appeared in an Atlanta newspaper, a clipping of which Aunt Lulu had sent Mother without any comment. It said that a Dr. Samuel Mosby Bridge, a locally prominent surgeon, had married the famous stage actress Lulu George. Was that the man who wouldn't have her in the long run? I asked Mother. She only remarked that Lulu had always been man crazy. And she drank far too much, she said, even in the early Follies days.

As he had given my mother, so my grandfather gave Lulu a sum of money. "To keep her off the streets," Mother had told me in an unguarded moment. From the disapproval in her voice, I had wondered if she meant Lulu was a natural-born whore.

"She sent me that postcard just before Christmas, you remember, the one with the holly wreath on it," she said. "I don't see why she couldn't come and stay for a bit. I could read between the lines that she's not doing a thing down there." After a pause, she said righteously, and I could hardly believe my ears though I *knew* she would say it, "After all, blood is thicker than water."

I imagined the thick, slow-moving viscosity of blood and the thin pure freedom of water.

"She might not want to come," I said.

"Then it will be a trip for you," she said promptly and with a certain airiness as though nothing much was at stake. "You might find a job and stay for a while. Of course, if you stay for more than a week, you'll *have* to find a job. I can't spare you much money."

She got up and went to the sink and filled a chipped iron-stone cup with water, drinking it in tiny sips like someone who has a fever. "Well, the soup's all cold now. I'll have to heat it up again."

"I don't want any."

"Neither do I," she said companionably, girlishly. As she put the cup down in its place by the sink, she sighed. "We didn't have much luck, Lulu and I," she said. She was looking past me through the door to the dining room, at the museum of my father's things on the table and in the cabinet. She started guiltily. "Oh, but there's you, of course."

"I don't want to be anybody's luck," I said roughly. I didn't mean exactly that. It was the falseness in her voice I couldn't bear at that moment. But if I had told her so, said it as plainly as I reported a cigarette burn in a cabin mattress, or a broken flush in a toilet, or that the Ford's right rear tire was worn smooth, it would have been as though a lawless stranger had joined our conversation.

There was as much ritual between us as in that of any church service. Like such a ritual, it served to evoke and celebrate an invisible deity, the blood of family connection, from the scalding heat of which our falseness gave us some protection. The news of my father's death had made the most negligibly spoken word, even a sigh, strike me like a blow. It was only eight o'clock. I was exhausted.

"You're a touch coldhearted," she said wistfully.

I stifled an impulse to protest. It would do no good. She was doing what she always did when life sharpened in our house. She was retreating into pathos.

"Do you think it's easy for me to let you go?" she demanded in a tremulous voice. "We are all frail barks, Helen."

She would not have extended such tolerance of frailty to Bernice, though I could hardly blame her for that. Tolerance is easy enough if you exclude from it everyone you despise.

"We were speaking of Lulu," she continued in a rather aloof voice, gathering up her dignity like a shawl. "If you could persuade her—I'm not at all sure I could—to spend some time with me."

"You can't persuade drunks to do anything," I said.

"Don't call her that!" she protested. "It's such a hateful word," she added with a touch of apology. She fell silent and covered her breasts with her plump arms.

We hadn't seen my aunt for years, not since I was fourteen and we had gone to Albany, where Lulu was playing Nora in a road company production of *A Doll's House*. She had treated us to a late supper in a hotel restaurant. In the gloomy, echoing room at a large round table covered with a cloth that was not clean, Aunt Lulu, I recalled, had kept her gaze steadily on the entrance to the dining room, as though waiting for an important guest. She had the loudest, deepest voice I had ever heard in a woman. I couldn't see any resemblance between the two sisters. Lulu's red hair started up from her forehead like a fire. My mother's hair was fair and orderly above her wide brow. I remembered that I had wondered if they were really sisters. That doubt suddenly returned.

I was on the point of asking her if there had been some scandal in the family she had kept from me—but she was weeping again, making no effort this time to stanch her tears.

"Oh, Mother! I know . . . but he's been gone so long! Forever!"

At that moment, I heard a car's motor. Headlights swept across the kitchen window. My mother said, "Why *do* they come so late? Why do people roam about all over the place when they should be home in their own beds!"

"Business for us," I reminded her.

"Yes. Yes, of course. And life must go on. Did you throw out those nasty-smelling flowers in the front bedroom?"

I had been on my way to dispose of the flowers that morning when I'd heard the postman and gone to get the mail instead.

"I'll do it now," I said. She was drying her face with a dish towel. I saw the curve of her short strong fingers as she gripped the towel for a second before she let it drop on the back of a chair. She smiled at me bravely. I glimpsed her small white teeth. I thought—she'll live a long time.

"Ready," she said.

CHAPTER

TWO

Matthew said, on the night before I left, "We've been going together a long time. We could get married." While he spoke I looked at his lips thinking how, when we made love, we got in each other's way.

I felt cruel yet pure when I told him it could not be; a life together was out of the question. He appeared more irritated by my declaration than brokenhearted. When I observed as much, he said, "A broken heart is *very* irritating, Helen," and he smiled with such melancholy sweetness, I felt I had not appreciated him until this moment of parting, not that it could matter to me anymore.

Only my mother's slow turning away from the front door, the hand with which she had been waving to me now resting on her brow where she held it so it covered her eyes, had postponed briefly the quickening of my senses which, once I was on the train, imparted to the most ordinary things I saw and touched an almost unbearable realness—the heavy cutlery of the dining car, the green baize of my window seat, which was as prickly as teasel, a thin, small wool blanket, new, nearly weightless, dropped on my lap by a porter as dusk fell, the grit on the surface of the window against which I pressed my forehead to stare out at the passing landscape, the waxen feel of paper cones which I filled with tepid drinking water from a brass tap in an alcove like a niche for a saint's statue at the end of the car.

It was as though the whole visible world—the train and the mysterious, continuously disappearing landscape through which it traveled—had been shaped by the blade of a knife, so sharply did I perceive it all. I dropped into sleep, exhausted, like a stone cast into a deep pond.

In the middle of the night, I was awakened by an infant crying in the seat in front of me. Its wet, mournful face appeared through the dark tangle of its mother's hair as she lifted it up, then lowered it until its head rested on her shoulder. It nestled there, sucked briefly at her neck and fell back to sleep, sliding from my view.

It was close and heavy in the car, as if the fleshly essences of the sleeping passengers were slowly thickening the air like arrowroot. The light was dim, flickering. Here and there along the aisle, a slack leg sprawled outward, an arm hung from an armrest, the hand and fingers slightly curled. The faces I could see were soft, so unguarded, so homely in sleep. Through the window I saw the vast waste of a swamp stretching to the border of the imprisoning darkness. Across the waste fled a double, a ghost train, its squares of light traveling in the opposite direction, north.

I could not imagine, could not visualize the emptiness of the corpse's face, that face I had last seen from my bedroom window years ago as my father had looked up once and for a long moment stared at the house as though he was trying to recognize it but failing to. I had watched him walk away from the empty stable. He had been wearing a dark-gray fedora, the brim aslant across his forehead. He carried a large suitcase in one hand, an unlit cigarette in the other. I had already heard the idling of a car motor on the road, probably the taxi from Poughkeepsie that would drive him to the train. As a rule, he took the car.

I had guessed he wouldn't come back that time—or was that what I always suspected? He did not see me at the window, and I remember how dreamily I waved at him, a private ceremony of my own.

He could lift me up with one arm until my cheek rested against his. My mother had said, "He'll come home. Let him get the restlessness out of his system . . . men are like that when they're down in the dumps."

In the house, a week ago, I could not have confessed to myself the pain of this now irrevocable loss for which the other parting had been only a rehearsal. I could not have given my mother such a chance to exercise her appalling gift for accommodation.

I wept now, between stations, nowhere, among the sleeping strangers. When I felt the fit of grief abating, I found myself trying to sustain it as though it were a kind of bliss I could not bear to relinquish. I spoke to myself some lines from a sonnet of Edna St. Vincent Millay's that had once stirred me: "Your face is like a chamber where a king / dies of his wounds, untended and alone . . . " But to my bewilderment, even as I silently pronounced the word *wounds*, I felt lifted up as if by a current of buoyant air, as if I were riding Felicity once again, out of sight of my mother and my father.

CHAPTER

THREE

For nearly a week, I wandered the streets of New Orleans, often not returning until evening to a small hotel on upper Canal Street where I had a room. One night, I fell onto the bed and into sleep before I had undressed, and woke at dawn to feel my clothes twisted around me like soft ropes. I had no urge to struggle free but lay still, hearing, I imagined, the city breathing like a great warm animal curled and drowsing within the curve of the Mississippi River.

One afternoon I stared through a restaurant window at a man sitting alone at a table, his long legs stretched out and crossed at the ankles, one hand in his trouser pocket, the other just reaching up to smooth back a lock of dark hair that had fallen over his forehead. He saw me looking at him and he smiled, a smile so alluring and intimate that it shattered the observer's detachment—or else a vague presumption I had become invisible—that had kept me safe, until that moment, from loneliness in this strange place. I walked on quickly.

The air smelled of ripe peaches and unknown flowers and, faintly, of something brackish, watery, and, in the French Market, of a kind of coffee to which chicory gave a bracing bitter sting. I drank a cup of it there, my elbow on the narrow marble counter of a small café, and gazed through the window at the stalls outside, dozens upon dozens of them, holding vegetables and fish and fruit I had not seen before. I had grown up in a country of turnips and potatoes, of food that grew hidden in the ground—or else my mother's reluctant cooking made it seem so.

Sellers and buyers spoke in a tangle of accents that were as indolent and balmy as the air. A jailhouse rose at one end of the market. In an alley that passed by it, I picked up an unsealed letter, the envelope marked with heel prints, no stamp, the address printed in pencil. I stared up at the barred windows of the jail sure the envelope had been dropped from one of them. I put it in my pocketbook, telling myself I would mail it for a poor prisoner but knowing I'd probably read it first.

Day after day, I postponed going in search of Aunt Lulu at the address she had sent my mother on the postcard. I had, several times, passed the building where she must live on Royal Street, averting my eyes from it.

In the late afternoons, I went to the river, where I watched colored men loading cargo, carrying their burdens on their backs and heads along wharves, up gangplanks, into the holds of ships. After, I went into the old quarter, the Vieux Carré, where dusk filled the streets as slowly as a dark honey poured from the sky. It was like moving among the rooms and corridors of a palace where boisterous preparations were under way for a party. Music resounded from the open entrance to a jazz club on Bourbon Street. I stood and looked at the colored jazzmen whose derbies tipped rakishly over their brows; they huddled together on a small platform held up, it seemed, by the thick cigarette smoke, their instruments shining like streaks of gold in their dark-skinned hands.

When I paused outside such a place, a man passing by might speak to me softly, insidiously, offering and requesting sexual delight. I was surprised to feel a remote sympathy toward such a man, more than I had felt for Matthew when his cold and clumpish hands clung to my breasts as though they were pendant ornaments I had put on for the occasions of our meetings.

I had not seen as many colored people in all my life as I passed on the streets during any afternoon. There was a colored section in Poughkeepsie where train porters, servants or laborers lived in small unpainted houses. A colored handyman had worked among the carpenters who had erected Mother's cabins. During the meal break, he had gone off by himself, hunkered down behind the trunk of a maple tree and taken from a paper sack a large brown biscuit. The other men got water from Mother who, as she proffered the glass to a fellow, made a gesture of it, wiping the glass with a small embroidered linen towel, smiling, one foot extended daintily. The colored man went to a pump near the tack room and drank there from a tin cup he took from the paper sack that contained his biscuit and, it seemed, nothing more.

Mother admired Marian Anderson, the Negro singer—she

was a fellow performer, after all—and praised Mrs. Roosevelt for resigning from the Daughters of the American Revolution when they refused to let Miss Anderson sing in Constitution Hall in Washington. She said colored people smelled different from white people, although she was sure Miss Anderson bathed often and was very clean.

I followed the colored worker around one afternoon. All I could smell were wood shavings and creosote. His grimness held my attention, it was so unavailingly itself; he never smiled, hardly spoke. His mouth was like a large budding flower slightly flattened by an invisible net. Late in the day, he suddenly looked right at me. "Leave me be!" he said in a low but distinct voice. I don't know why I had imagined he couldn't see me. I was shocked by the sudden awareness that he could, more so than by his stark words, and I ran into the house, my face flaming.

I didn't write to Mother. It would break the spell, evoke the house and cabins and empty stable, which I envisaged as being bathed in a drab gray light. I knew it was a false picture.

It was this first real privacy in my life I wanted to preserve, a voluptuous inner silence hardly disturbed by the few words I uttered to order food or to return the greetings of the desk clerk. But on Monday, six days after I had arrived in New Orleans, I was forced to think about money. When I counted out the bills I had left, I felt a thrill of fear to be so close to destitution.

I had eaten when I was hungry. I had bought sandals and a cotton dress and skirt at Fountain's, a department store on lower Canal Street, and it was there I returned, hoping to get a job. The man who did the hiring seemed less interested by far in my dry-goods-store experience in Poughkeepsie than he was in my dress. He leaned toward me and pinched the cloth of the sleeve. I noted lumpy little islands of talcum powder on his cheeks and jowls, as though he'd dusted himself with it before drying his face. "You buy that dress here?" he asked.

When I said I had, he observed with satisfaction that he was sure he had recognized it. I suspected it was out of that satisfaction that he hired me, even though I said I hadn't sold ladies' undergarments before. "There's not a whole lot to learn," he said loftily.

I was determined to find a place to live in the Vieux Carré, the French Quarter. The desk clerk at the hotel recommended instead a boardinghouse near St. Charles Avenue. It would be more suitable, he said. "The Quarter's full of fruits," he explained.

The way he pronounced *fruits* in his papery, rather hooting voice, along with his fatuous look of expressing the whole world's opinion, made me burst into laughter. Although I had not heard that word used as he had used it, I knew instantly what it referred to. (I wondered if one could always grasp the meaning of animadversions, no matter how unfamiliar, by someone's tone of voice; I wondered if there were not thousands of tones, far more than there were words—their meaning experienced but yet to be shaped by language.)

When I was eight, my father's elder brother, my uncle Morgan, had died in an automobile accident on the Boston Post Road while driving north to visit us. He had been expected for supper. He had telephoned to say he'd been held up in the city and would be late. I had gone to bed by the time the second call, from the police, came.

"We only had each other," my father said after the funeral. I had gone to it because my father had said I must be there. My mother had wept and said I was too young to go to a funeral. I had wanted to look at my uncle, to see the change from life to death—unspeakable mystery. But the coffin was closed because Uncle Morgan had been so mangled by the accident. When I begged my mother to have the coffin opened, she spoke to me with unusual harshness. Only primitive people had the vile custom of viewing dead bodies, she said.

Later that year, I was fooling around in Felicity's stall, eavesdropping without much interest, at first, on a conversation between a stableboy and an electrician who had come to do some work. Yes, Mr. Bynum was a good man to work for, the boy told the electrician. Especially now that that pansy brother had kicked the bucket. The electrician had muttered something; the stableboy had said Mister Queer had tried to back him into a corner more than twice.

It was no effort to recall the alarm I had felt in the warm dark stall; that same alarm had been part of what provoked my laughter at the desk clerk, a sense of a fearsome undertow of rage and incomprehension he had expressed in word, in voice. My mother planted pansies in the spring. In grammar school, we were sexual louts, guffawing at certain words: *breast*, *hair*, *hoary*, *thing*. *Pansy* was new. At last, I spoke to my father.

"My brother was a homosexual man," he said to me gravely. "That's what they meant. I can't explain it. I don't know how. It means that he loved men."

"But he loved me," I protested.

He smiled. "Yes, he did," he agreed. "Don't pay much attention to what people say. Then, someday, you'll find out what you think yourself. Try to go to what is new as innocently as you can—let the surprise of it take you first."

The desk clerk was fussing with the keys that hung from a board on the wall behind the desk. He knocked several to the floor, where they banged and clattered. He had taken offense at my laughter. I nearly told him that it had been his voice that had made me laugh, not what he'd said, as though that distinction would endear me to him.

"You don't even know what a *fruit* is," he said triumphantly, the keys gripped in his bony hand. I hesitated. But he was too dumb, so I replied that I guessed I didn't. He noticed the newspaper I had bought that morning, hoping I might find a room advertised in it.

"Girls reading newspapers!" he cried scornfully.

I wanted suddenly to fight with him, reduce him to a last component of himself—an extremely dim light bulb inside his skull. Just as suddenly my anger went. "I'm trying to learn how," I said, widening my eyes at him.

"Good luck," he said amiably, appeased.

I took the paper to a chair by the hotel entrance. Out of some lingering defiance, I looked intently at the front page before turning to the classified section. As I read of the Nazi capture of Yugoslav generals and the Greek government's escape to Crete after the collapse of the army, I glanced at the desk to see if the clerk was observing me. He was leaning on the counter. One hand supported his chin as he stared blankly at the hotel entrance, in the same posture in which I nearly always found him when I returned to the hotel.

I noticed that his arm, his hand, his head, were rocking very slightly back and forth as though a weak electrical current were being applied to some part of his person. He looked to be the embodiment of tedium. My expression of a wish to live in the Quarter had charged him with the momentary energy of contempt. Did he think about Germany? About Adolf Hitler and the Nazis? He was young enough to be drafted.

"They're forever quarreling over there—it won't come to anything," Mother had said when the Germans invaded Poland, and I had wondered aloud if there was going to be another world war.

Armies, generals, were passing into the dark. The desk clerk was vibrating with boredom. For a little while I sat there, torpid, bewildered by my intentions, the paper fallen across my lap.

I had not looked up Aunt Lulu. I had not done what I should have done this week. I wondered if that was to be my plan for the rest of my life.

After some passage of time I couldn't measure, I got up and went out of the hotel. After me, the clerk bawled, "Be good, yawl!"

The room I rented was the top floor of a small two-story building of old brick that stood in an untended garden behind a wooden house on St. Phillip Street. A staircase, little more than a ladder, led from the room down to a dark kitchen that smelled of pepper, and a tiny bathroom of still raw wood, evidently added to the building recently, which contained a toilet and a little bathtub like a round pot.

The room was drowned in morning light from its one window which faced the east. I glanced around it once. Something I had gathered up in that glance made my heart beat fast; I suddenly believed I would be happy.

The woman who had shown it to me waited below. I descended the stairs into the peppery, shadowed kitchen and she held open the screen door for me. A brick walk led to the back stairs of the main house. Plants and flowers grew everywhere in pleasant disarray. "Mostly gardenia," she said as I sniffed the air. She sat down on the circular rim of a fountain, its stone basin stained with patches of green and yellow. "It hasn't worked for years, but we like to sit around it in the evenings when there's a breeze."

I told her I loved the room. "The building used to be slave quarters," she said. "It needs fixing." I looked at the rosy brick, the nestlike granular pouches where plaster had crumbled and settled, and places where narrow laths showed through. "But it got to be beautiful," she said, "though it wasn't once."

Her name was Catherine Bruce, and I supposed her to be in her early thirties. The rent was eight dollars a week, and I could use the kitchen whenever I wanted to.

"That's the only bathroom," she said. "So we'll share that." She clasped one knee with her small square hands. "I live with Gerald Boyd. He's a poet. He's out at the market right now. He does all the cooking. Three mornings a week, I go do typing for a man who's writing a history of New Orleans." She smiled up at me as I stood in front of her. She told me these things bravely, as though it were a difficult matter to speak of them but honesty required it. She hadn't said she was married to the man who cooked, who was a poet.

"I'll go back to the hotel," I told her. "I better get my things, they might charge me for an extra day otherwise."

When I walked through the main house to the street, I noticed this time how bare it was, a living room, a bedroom, and another small room leading off it, in which I glimpsed a square table covered with sheets of paper. The furniture was plain; bed, wood chairs, a settee, a bookcase made of planks resting on bricks, and a round wooden table in front of the empty hearth of a small fireplace. I felt utterly strange to myself; even my voice as I said goodbye to Catherine seemed not to belong to me. And this spell of strangeness that had the quality of profound thought, the subject of which I couldn't consciously grasp, lasted all the way to the hotel and back, when I carried my suitcase up the short flight of stairs to my new room.

This time Catherine followed me and stood in the narrow doorway, her hands behind her back against the door frame. Her dark hair swung forward against her cheeks like the points of scimitars. She was wearing a tan blouse and soft, loose pants like pajamas. On her feet she wore some sort of braided leather slippers. Everything about her was singular to me, the quick fluent way she moved, the way her clothes and hair seemed so undevised yet eloquent of a quality about her nature I couldn't name but that could be suggested by certain words like *Shenandoah* or *Alabama*—but not *Poughkeepsie*. She looked as unfamiliar as the fruit I had seen in the stalls of the French Market. As I thought of that, the word *beautiful* slid into my mind. I was staring at her. She was smiling, allowing me to look at her. Perhaps it was time to turn away. I began to put underwear and stockings in the top drawer of a small bureau. I noticed the room. A worn clean towel hung from a hook near the door. There was a red coverlet on the bed, a light blanket at its foot. On the bureau stood a bright blue basin holding a ewer of the same color. Near where Catherine stood was a chair with a cane seat.

"I tried to make the room look like that," she said as she caught my eye. I looked at the wall toward which she had gestured. A framed print hung there, a reproduction of a painting of another room that looked much like the room we were in. "That's van Gogh's bedroom," she said. "I forgot to bring you a mirror. I'll hang it beside the window like it is in the painting. I love that room. It's so safe, although it wasn't for him."

She pushed herself away from the wall. "You can take a bath whenever you want, but the water is never really hot." She disappeared down the stairs. From the kitchen she called up, "If there's anything you want . . . " I heard the screen door close.

I looked at the reproduction. I recalled all at once, in a soft explosion of memory, where I had seen it before. It had been tacked to a board in my high school classroom next to a window from which I could see the foothills of the Catskill Mountains across the Hudson. Now I had walked right into the painting, leaving behind that other life whose horizon had been those foothills.

I couldn't postpone going in search of Aunt Lulu another day, another hour. I sat down on the bed and began to look in my pocketbook for her postcard. I found the letter I had picked up from the street near the jail, the gum of its flap now stuck to Lulu's card. It was addressed to Julette Fortier in Baton Rouge. It had no salutation.

> How come you was so hard with me? I be here so long without your comfort. How come you didin bring me smokes? Didin I ast you for them? You blame me and blame me and blame me. Bring smokes next time. I'm dying with nothing to do to pass my time.

It was signed *Albert*.

I licked my finger and drew it across the dried glue of the flap and pressed until the envelope was sealed. When I stood the letter against the basin on the bureau, Julette Fortier seemed to claim the room as her own, to be one with the blue ewer sitting in its basin like a plump waterfowl, with the brightness of the red coverlet on the bed, the sturdiness of the legs of the small chair. I had read her letter; she had taken my room away from me. I stuffed the letter back in my pocketbook. Then I combed my hair, looking at sections of my head in a tortoise-shell-backed mirror my mother had given me, and set off, without further excuses for delaying, for Royal Street.

CHAPTER

FOUR

Against high walls that hid gardens whose flower scents filled the air, the tendrils and leaves of climbing vines cast shadows that lengthened moment by moment. The Quarter murmured at this hour like many dovecotes. People moved indolently, paused, lingered on a corner, and I half expected someone would come to take them by the arm and lead them home, or to a garden where they might take their ease. In the entrance to shops on Royal Street, clerks stretched and yawned. Through a window I glimpsed ivory elephants in file on a narrow ledge of dusty black velvet and below them, in gilt or tarnished silver frames, tinted drawings of quadroon balls.

The Royal Street streetcars rumbled along, slow as sleepy mammals, and they had names printed on boards attached to their sides. I kept pace for a long block with *Piety*.

The building whose number Aunt Lulu had written on the

postcard she had sent to my mother, and which I had passed by several times on my walks, was like a derelict ship that had run aground. Along its second-story balcony ran an undecipherable sentence written in the ornate script of a wrought-iron grille. The arched entranceway, its doors flung back against the inner walls, reminded me of a stable. The wooden floor I walked upon, scored as if by hooves, gave on to a stone courtyard dominated by a huge fountain. Its marble basin was dry, and rising from its center, the rusted tip of a pipe poking up from among her marble curls, was the statue of a girl poised on one foot, leaning forward as though in flight, her outstretched arms and hands turned to branches and twigs.

I had been aware of the sound of moving water, but looking at the fountain, I had not believed my ears. Now I saw water spreading from beneath a wall in one dark corner and flowing across the bottom steps of a broad flight of stairs, to the base of another wall under which it had worn a small channel. A rough wooden plank bridged the submerged steps, its lower end causing an eddy in the water, which gave it the calm appearance of a rural stream with its small events of hidden stones or logs. A bluish watery light glimmered from patchily whitewashed walls; how soon would they give way and this old wreck sink? It was silent except for the peaceable murmur of the water, eerie, dreamlike.

I walked the plank and up the stairs. High double doors, the kind I associated with servants ushering visitors into drawing rooms, lined a long corridor. On the wall at the side of the first pair of doors, one of which was slightly ajar, *Miss Lulu George* was printed in green crayon.

I pushed open the door slowly. My eyes were dazzled by a
yellow glow, the last flaring of the sun before dusk, pouring
through dusty windows that opened out onto the balcony I had
seen from the street. I had the sense of a weight pressing down
from above, an extreme darkness. The room was immense, circular. I looked up. The domed ceiling so far above was a blue-
black sky across which were flung, like fishermen's nets, the
constellations, each star as distinct as a white thorn. I heard a
gargling noise that ended in a breathy whistle. The gargle began
once again and I lowered my head. A tall young man was looking at me intently, his finger against his mouth, warning me not
to speak. He was standing at the foot of a big bed whose occupant I did not, at first, look at, though I was aware of a body
lying there and that the noise I had heard was issuing from that
body.

The young man's thick feathery hair was silver. He seemed to
be at the very core of that yellow glow which in its slow ebbing
revealed on the dusty floor crumpled garments, a pair of
stained peach-colored high-heeled shoes, an empty liquor bottle and an alligator purse like my mother's gaping near the foot
of the bed, some change spilled across it. But these objects,
though I noted them, held at that moment no meaning at all.

Often I had puzzled about where in myself a concentrated
sentient self was really lodged, the one that ceaselessly spoke—
perhaps in dreams, too—and judged and directed my attention to this or that—the self that thought it thought. I felt now
as though that thing, that being or consciousness, had taken
possession of every cell of my person and that all of it had settled in my eyes, and everything in the room fell away into a void

except the man's silver hair, his straight black eyebrows, the silencing finger that flattened his wide thin mouth. I wonder how long I would have stood there, rapt, if he hadn't gestured suddenly toward the bed.

Collapsed upon it, a sheet drawn up to her navel, naked as far as I could tell, was Aunt Lulu. Her eyes were squeezed shut as though she were keeping them closed with conscious effort, but her mouth was slackly open. The stained pillow upon which her red hair lay clumped and matted was without a case. From under the sheet, her pale, long, narrow feet protruded. Her breasts flowed sideways against her upper arms, and her nipples resembled dusty raspberries. As I went toward the bed, I could smell her stale flesh, the sour acridness of liquor on her breath. Her nakedness embarrassed me dreadfully. I leaned over her to pull up the sheet, but the young man instantly caught my hand and shook his head. I backed toward the door, wanting only to get away from him, my aunt, this strange room.

I had known long ago that my aunt was what my mother had called a bohemian, that she lived without ordinary restraints. But I hadn't had the least notion of what that was all about. Now, the very idea that I had traveled south to persuade this great red drunken creature to help run a humble cabin business in a cold northern rural place was so ludicrous I suspected Mother had played a monstrous trick on me—she must have known how far Lulu had fallen, how impossible the plan was— and I felt fevered with resentment.

I supposed the young man was my aunt's lover, or one of her lovers. But I was mortified for a reason other than my aunt's

bared breasts and the particularly intimate and powerfully un-
settling sight—because *he* was there—of her nipples. He must
have thought me either deranged, or worse, a yokel without
manners, to look at him as I had, and for so long. Of course, it
was all because of his silver hair.

He was following me, walking almost noiselessly. I went into
the corridor, rehearsing a letter in my mind to Mother. In the
first sentence, I lied and said I hadn't been able to track down
Aunt Lulu. In the second sentence, I declared her a hopeless
sot. The letter vanished, the thought of having to go home took
its place. I was in despair. The young man stepped out from behind the doors.

"We mustn't wake her," he said in a low voice. "It's the first
time in days she's really slept. She's been drunk for a week and
roaring."

His white frayed shirt was open at the collar and his neck
rose strongly from it. He glanced back into the room, then
turned to me.

"You must know—you must know it now anyhow, that there
isn't going to be a repertory theater," he said gravely. "When
she sobers up, she pastes signs all over the place. Where did you
see one?" He frowned. "I thought I'd taken them all down.
Well, it's a joke in the Quarter. 'Oh! Lulu must have sobered
up!' That's what people say when they see those signs. That's
why I came to her a couple of months ago. I thought she might
give me a job making sets or something like that."

Up close, I noticed that even his small tight ears had a silvery
cast.

"My mother's hair turned gray early, too," he said simply and as though accustomed to having to account for it. But he touched his head rather self-consciously.

"I didn't come for a job," I said. My voice surprised me; I felt I'd been silent for weeks. And there was a faint tremor in it. "I'm Lulu's niece, Helen Bynum."

"She told me she had a niece. I wasn't sure . . . she makes up so much. I thought you were an actress looking for a job." He took a pack of cigarettes from his shirt pocket and held it out to me. I shook my head. I felt such an intense and peculiar shyness that I shrank from touching his cigarette pack as though it would have been the same as his skin.

"My mother, her sister, wants Lulu to go live with her for a while. My mother rents out cabins up near Poughkeepsie. You know where that is? My father died recently."

"I'm sorry," he said somewhat mechanically. He was smoking, looking past my shoulder down the stairs. I knew he had not really taken me in. He had some private nervousness of his own that was distracting him, about Lulu, I assumed.

"My parents haven't lived together for years," I told him. "He was living with a woman in California."

He sighed and leaned against the wall near Lulu's crayoned name. Suddenly he bent to the doors, listened, then fell back as though weary. "I thought she said something intelligible," he explained. "She makes some amazing sounds when she's like this."

I wanted to laugh and I wanted to go away. The reason that had brought me to New Orleans was lying in a drunken stupor in that singular room. I wanted to think about it all; I wanted to discover a *way* of thinking about it that would allow me to stay in the south.

"What kind of room is that? Are all the rooms along here like it?"

"It was a ballroom in the last century when one family owned this place. It was a mansion then. Did you notice the ceiling? The constellations?"

I nodded.

"I'm Len Mayer," he said. "I'm from Chicago." He stepped on his cigarette butt, picked it up, pinched it and dropped it in his trouser pocket. "I've been here only a few months. Really, I'm just waiting to be drafted. I'm 1-A." He looked at me directly, his face somber. "I couldn't stand waiting at home. Are you in the Quarter?"

"Yes," I replied firmly, and as I imagined my new room I felt light with exaltation, free. "I just found a place. I'm renting it from a woman, Catherine Bruce." I nearly told him about my job, but I feared I would seem childish, happy in the manner of a child.

Len Mayer smiled. "Catherine." He pronounced her name fondly. "She lives with Gerald Boyd. Everyone in the Quarter knows him. His wife is a Catholic. She won't let him go so he can marry Catherine."

"Is my aunt drunk all the time?"

"She goes on benders. Between times, she's pretty sober. She gets a check from some trust now and then. When that arrives, she dolls herself all up and stops drinking and starts to plan the theater I mentioned. Something always starts her up drinking again. Howard Meade—you met him yet? He owns the bookstore, and he'll say something that offends her. Or else her ex-husband will come around."

"We knew she got married. She sent us a newspaper clipping. Mother guessed there was a divorce when she never wrote about her husband."

"That's Sam Bridge. He's a doctor. He's doing his military service now at Fort Benning. He comes to the Quarter whenever he gets leave. Too often. He knows Gerald Boyd, too. I wish he'd stay away from Lulu, but he always drops by. They weren't married for more than a year or so, I think. I don't believe he cares a thing about her. Why does he want to see her? I don't know. Afterwards, she gets drunk."

"You know a lot about her," I said. I felt nettled, oppressed. I'd been so lifted up, happy, thinking about my room. Didn't anything last more than a minute or two? "I don't see her settling in with my mother in Poughkeepsie and cleaning out cabins and the two of them drawing up chairs in the evening to listen to *Amos 'n' Andy* on the radio."

"No," he agreed.

"Did she ever talk to you about us—besides just saying she had relatives?" I was wondering how I could get him to tell me about himself and Lulu. Did she, could she support him? Did he live with her?

"I've got a room over at Pirates Alley," he said.

His hair. Now his living arrangements. How did he know what I was thinking? It probably showed on my face. Could there be a face one could develop over time, an unreadable one for use in the world? I had hardly been in the world; there had hardly been any strangers in my life. It was Mother who had dealt with the guests who rented the cabins while I looked them over from behind a window.

"I get work when I can," Len was saying. "There are plenty of restaurants in the Quarter." Suddenly, I found him irritating. He was smiling self-deprecatingly.

"But did she——"

"——Yes, oh, yes!" he responded hastily. I felt bad; I'd managed to make him feel ashamed, probably for talking about himself. "She told me she had a sister who married a rich turfman. And they were both in the Follies, she and your mother. I believed that . . . about the Follies and her acting because she has photographs to prove it."

He looked impressed as he must have done when my aunt showed him those photographs. "But she does tell such tales," he went on. "She has that liar's trick, you know, looking away, then back at you to see how her story is going over? I hope you don't mind my saying so. She's got charm, you know. I mean—— she lies like a ten-year-old and she has the charm of a child—— though you might not believe it at the moment. She'll suddenly get enthusiastic about something. And these great plans. And she's like hope personified——just because it's so awful for her most of the time. Sorry. I'll shut up. I really do feel so sorry about her——what's happening."

"I don't mind your talking about her," I said. It wasn't true. "But has she ever mentioned me?"

"I think so," he replied, frowning slightly as though trying to recall. "I do think so." I knew he wanted to spare my feelings. I was sure she hadn't said one word about me.

"She even invented a baby," he said. "Sam's child, who died

because Sam was out with some woman and Lulu didn't realize the baby's fever was dangerously high."

"Why would she make up something so dreadful? And didn't she know no one would believe her?"

"I don't think she worries about being believed," he answered. "It's wonderful, in a way, that she doesn't give a damn. Sam says feeling tragic makes her happy."

We both started at a loud groan from the ballroom. A second later, my aunt howled, "Lennie! Lennie!"

He ran into the room. I followed reluctantly. Lulu's eyes were still tightly closed, but she was sitting upright. I saw a line of reddish down, like the palest of scars, on her swollen belly. Her head began to sink forward until she seemed to be staring closely, crazily, at her own breasts. Len Mayer put his hand on her head and pressed steadily until she collapsed back onto the bed. Her lips trembled in an infant's gassy smile.

We waited. Len switched on a tiny cone-shaped bulb in a tin wall-bracket. The light made little difference in that huge room. But shadows suited it. I glanced up at the ceiling.

The stars in the constellations seemed to glint more sharply than they had earlier. Lamps had been lit on Royal Street, and I could see worn strips of tar paper lying on the uneven floor of the balcony. Below one of the windows stood a narrow cot strewn with clothes. There were two wooden chairs of the simplest sort near the cot, and a small bureau of dark wood on which sat a saucepan. A door across from the bed was open. It revealed a space no larger than a closet; it contained a small sink, a shelf that held a hot plate, a few stacked dishes and utensils, and some other objects I couldn't identify from where I stood. Another door in the curving wall might have concealed a bathroom.

Len stirred and sighed. I listened to my aunt's breathing, loud but regular. I noticed some suitcases beneath the bed. He came to me and touched my arm and nodded at the doors. As we stepped out into the corridor, I asked him about the stream in the hall. It came from a bar around the corner, he told me— it was because of some trouble with the plumbing the owner had never fixed. It always diminished in the evening but was in full spate every morning.

"We could have a beer in the bar, Murphy's," he suggested tentatively.

"What about her?"

"I think she'll be out now for a while. She always yells once or twice. Even when she's passed out, she wants people to know she's around. She'll come out of it some time tonight."

"You know so much about her."

He turned his silver head away from me and took a step toward the doors. But he turned back almost at once. "There is more to her than that," he said. I waited. He didn't add anything, didn't say what more there was to her.

Was he a kind of servant? Young men, a worker from Pough-keepsie or a guest, had often looked amused by my mother. Was it because they had recognized her former allure, and was their amusement a kind of tribute to it?

Aunt Lulu was not alluring, at least not in her present condition. Did Len feel uneasy because I was there, a witness,

someone to whom he felt he owed an explanation of his presence and his familiar way with her? Her nakedness! My cheeks
grew hot.

His wrists were as thin as a boy's. His fingers were narrow,
oval at their tips. Beneath his cuffs, I glimpsed a delicate cover-
ing of dark hair.

"I think I'd better go back to my room. I'm not quite moved
in," I said, making up a reason for going that was a matter of
trivial efficiency had it been true. I didn't want him to think I
wanted to get away from him, away from the sluttish old ballroom in which my relative slept, reeking of drink. But I did. It
was all beyond my experience and I was sated, queasy with the
newness of it all.

"I'll come back later this evening," I said, not sure I would.

"All right," he said. "That might be better." I heard the relief
in his voice, and I was disappointed.

The stream in the hall had become a trickle. I didn't need to
use the plank.

In the street, freed from daylight constraint by the dark, people
talked loudly, boisterously. As I walked down Royal, I thought
of those two sisters, of the younger one whom I'd lived with all
my life except for these last few days- —did she have the least
idea who it was she had sent me to, to bring back to her?

I could imagine my mother calling Lulu a madcap even as my
aunt tore the cabins apart, pulled down the house around her,
confounded her with the pure anarchic awfulness of her real
sister's presence. Aunt Lulu dreamed too, was an inventor of

tales, with a difference. Vanish! I commanded my two living relatives.

I spoke Len's name aloud. Tears formed in my eyes. An emotion nearly unbearable in its intensity brought me to a halt at the corner of St. Phillip. I could not name it. But hadn't he been neutral, like a doctor or a nurse, when we were looking down at her? He had said there was more to her than *that*. Was that a lover's defensiveness? Or had he only tried to be just to her?

"My record of fairness is as clean as a whistle," Mother often claimed. It was simply a matter of "overlooking" things, things, I had come to realize, she kept the most careful accounts of. But Len had been trying to do Lulu justice. That was not my mother's way.

Two young men paused and looked at me questioningly. I started to walk on. One tipped his straw hat and murmured, "Pleasant evening . . . " I went quickly to the Boyd house.

When I entered the front room, I saw a small thin man with dark hair sitting in one of the straight chairs, his eyes closed, a copy of *Life* magazine on his lap, one hand preventing it from slipping to the floor. In front of the hearth, the round table had been set with three places, plates, knives and forks. There was no tablecloth.

My mother would have pulled a face at that. She clothed everything. If she found me undressing a doll, she would clasp my hands tightly. "No, no. Naked we come, but dressed we stay," she would say. Remembering that now, I wondered what she told herself about her showgirl costumes.

The man, who I knew must be Gerald Boyd, looked to be in

his mid-forties. His plaid shirt was buttoned up to his neck. His hair was dark and thick above his heavily lined forehead. He rested lightly on the surface of sleep like a leaf on a pond. I stood motionless, afraid I might wake him. Although his breathing was deep and regular, and his face was so still in its repose, there was an air of readiness about him.

He cleared his throat faintly and opened his eyes, looking up at me and smiling. "I'm not truly asleep," he said in a low voice with an undertone of hoarseness like that of a person recovering from a cold. He held his free hand out to me, the other keeping hold of the magazine. I took it and felt the hard pads of his warm palm against my own.

"I'm Helen Bynum. The room . . ."

"You're going to be our boarder," he said. "You'll excuse me if I don't get up. I'm supposed to take it slow whenever I get a moment."

"He's cooked our supper, so he has to rest now. He's made us gumbo," Catherine said as she came into the room carrying three glasses and a small bottle of gin, all of which she placed on the table. "We've been saving this drink. Professor Graves, the man I work for, gave it to me at New Year's. Every time we thought to open it, Gerald said, 'Let's wait—there'll be a better moment,' and the moments came and went. You were the first person showed up to see the room. So it was meant to be opened now. A man came this afternoon—"

She poured a small amount of gin into each glass and handed one to Gerald, then one to me. "—I told him the room was taken, but he wanted to see it anyhow, see what he'd lost out on, and when he did, he said he would've hated living over a kitchen and having to smell food cooking. He was thin as a stick." She grinned.

"Sour grapes," said Gerald.

I liked gin. Matthew and I sometimes drank it from his tarnished flask, sitting in his old Buick on cold nights on the hill above his house, looking down on the light he'd left on when he went to work in the morning. It glowed, amber, in the parlor bay window, and all the romance between us was held in those moments like a butterfly still alive in the net that has captured it.

Gerald sipped his gin slowly. He didn't have an invalid's look. The *Life* magazine slipped to the floor. I stooped to pick it up and he said, "It'll be all right there. I found it on the sidewalk this morning. See the heel prints on it? You ever look at it? There's something strange about the pictures. They remind you of their subjects like you're reminded of people who are dead. Catherine says you come from way up north. I'd like to see the north. I've never been out of Louisiana."

He stood up slowly. As he began to move chairs to the table, I noticed he had a slight limp. "I can do that," I offered.

"Oh, I can do lots of things though I have this heart ailment," he said. "It's only that I have to make choices about which things I do." Catherine had gone to the kitchen and returned carrying a steaming pot, which she set down in the center of the table.

From the narrow mantel of the fireplace, she took a candle in a yellow saucer and put it next to the pot. Gerald lit a kitchen match with his thumbnail. "I wish you wouldn't do that," she murmured. He was smiling somewhat absently, hearing something he was used to. He touched the wick with the burning match. It flamed and flared up, and their faces, not young, not old, nearly touching, were transfigured, a tableau of grave, private love. They drew apart and looked at me. They didn't know what I'd seen, that still lingered about their eyes; they were as unconscious of it as meadow grass stirred by a breeze that has begun to subside.

I thought of the woman who wouldn't divorce Gerald. I thought of her seeing them as I just had; it would have crushed her. I trembled inwardly at some apprehension of the absolute unfairness of life.

"You ever eat okra before?" Gerald asked me as we sat down at the table. "I heard it takes getting used to."

They spoke about themselves. It was as though they unfolded maps of their lives: here is a hill, a village, a river, here are the crossroads.

"He's a poet now," Catherine had told me when I first saw my room. He had worked in an automobile assembly plant in Baton Rouge. A door fell on his foot and he lost two toes. He'd worked since he was a boy, and he'd written poems. A celebrated writer had taken a tour of the plant. Gerald had been his guide. "All the time I was explaining about the cars, I was thinking about my poems. And at the end, when he was about to leave, right after he said thanks and goodbye, I took hold of his jacket. I just shouted at him —'*Wait!*' "

Catherine said the celebrated writer had taken Gerald's poems to a publisher, and they were published and Gerald won a prize. "Pretty soon, I quit that place," he said. "And I came here to the Quarter, and my whole life changed."

Catherine came from Arizona to get away from home and from the university she had attended, where she could have had a teaching position. She found temporary jobs in New Orleans that barely paid her enough to keep going, and after a year it didn't feel like she'd left home, she was just treading water, she said. On the morning she decided to return to Arizona, she picked up the newspaper at the door of the boardinghouse where she'd been living. Gerald had placed an ad in it: *Writer needs typist*.

"I didn't put in *poet*," Gerald said. "*Writer* sounded more permanent and more like there might be enough money to pay someone."

"I would have answered it anyhow, if you had—and poets are the most permanent."

Gerald touched my arm. "You like the gumbo?"

"I like it. I just don't know what's in it."

"There's shrimp and crab," he said.

Catherine lit a cigarette. "I get to smoke in the evening," she said. "The Professor doesn't like me to while I'm working."

"We've been together three years," Gerald said. "My wife is Catholic and won't divorce me. I've got two grown children. Now and then the boy gets so mad he won't see me. Then he forgets to be mad. It's not his nature."

"We'll have coffee now," Catherine said.

There was a knock on the screen door, through which I discerned a large indistinct figure.

"Claude," Catherine said.

Gerald turned in his chair, looking pleased. "Come on in, Claude."

The man who stepped into the room was tall and solidly made. His large head was covered with a cap of light brown curls.

"Oh—you're at dinner," he said. "I'll come back another time."

"We're through. Have coffee with us."

"I only wanted to give you the book I was telling you about last week."

He stood for a moment at the door. He was so still, his body so quiet, he seemed to belong to an order other than the human one, mineral, perhaps, like marble. He was wearing a white linen suit, and as he held out the book, I caught the scent of lemon.

Gerald rose and took the book from him and put it on the table. It was called *Adolphe*, and it was by Benjamin Constant.

I felt a sudden confusion—was it about Hitler? Would Catherine and Gerald want to read a book about Hitler? And one whose title referred to him so familiarly by his first name?

Amidst all that was so unfamiliar—the pungent, ropy food that I had eaten greedily and with a faint revulsion, these people I had begun to love as suddenly as one starts out of sleep at a loud clap of thunder, the air in the room with its mingled smells of cooking, and flowers that must have opened in the dark in all the gardens of the Quarter—the book lay near my hand evoking an alien northern world, frozen, violent, and full of incomprehensible monstrous noise.

They were talking together. The book was bound in cream-colored paper. I opened it covertly, feeling against my finger the ragged edges of the paper on which it was printed. On the title page, I saw the original publication date, 1816, and on a further page, that it was in French. "Oh!" I exclaimed.

They looked at me inquiringly.

"Claude, this is our boarder, Helen Bynum," Catherine said. "And this is Claude de la Fontaine."

He held out his beautiful large hand, the skin as creamy as the color of the book. He gripped my hand, let it go instantly and said he must be off.

When he had gone, I said, "My God! I thought this book was about Adolph Hitler!"

Gerald burst into laughter.

"Of course, I can see now, there's an e on the *Adolphe*," I said sheepishly.

"Catherine's going to read it to me," he said. "She can read French—"

"—I used to."

When she brought us coffee, the same kind I had tasted in the small café near the French Market, they looked at me expectantly. It was my turn.

I didn't much want to talk. I wanted to go on listening to them. I thought of my life—water and hardtack. But as I began to relate the simple outline, their interest enveloped me, and watching their intent faces, I felt touched with eloquence, or as if I had suddenly discovered I could sing; and although so much was left out—I couldn't relive for them my life in its actuality, in its hours and minutes—as I told of a landscape, a house, the occupations of my mother and my father, my grandfather, the philosopher, who had become a purveyor of cough medicine, the stables where the horses stirred and rumbled, my father's departure, the building of the cabins, I heard, almost impersonally, that my narration was as singular as theirs, as coherent, resonating with all the moments that must remain unexpressed, sunk in time itself.

When I said that my mother had been one of those "glorified girls" in the Follies, Gerald clapped his hands, and Catherine laughed aloud with surprise, and when I spoke the name of my aunt whom I'd been sent to bring back to my mother, she cried, "Lulu! But we know her! The doctor she was married to is an old friend of ours. Sam Bridge. He took care of Gerald when he was so sick."

Across her calm face, in her cool gray eyes, there was a fleeting look of alarm as though she'd heard a distant cry. The candle had become a stub. The flame flickered and went out. I felt a bit sunk, uncertain.

"My mother wants Aunt Lulu to go live with her," I said. "She was too drunk to speak when I saw her today. A young man was there."

"That would be Len," Gerald said.

He must have read something in my face, some disappointment. I wished it hadn't showed. But it was a blow. His knowing at once who it was proved the connection between my aunt and Len.

"He's a very nice fellow," Gerald said.

"So many people in the Quarter come from somewhere else," Catherine said softly. "It's like we've all been floated down here on the river and deposited—like silt on the delta."

"Is she drunk a lot?" I asked.

Gerald looked at me. His cheeks were red, his eyes black; he looked the picture of health. Perhaps Aunt Lulu's appearance had been deceptive, too.

"She is," he said, with something in his voice I heard as merciful.

"Len told me that the doctor, your friend, comes to visit her and that sets off her drinking."

"I don't believe she needs much to set it off," Gerald said. "It's true Sam is a bit of a rake, yet I think he really worries about her."

Catherine snorted and shook her head. "I'm grateful to him and I can't help it that I'm fond of him. But I know he goes to see Lulu to show himself he can still provoke and upset her," she said.

"Catherine, he's not so cruel!"

"Well—maybe not. But he certainly doesn't worry about her."

I stood up. "What time is it, do you know? I have to go back and see her. And I start my job at Fountain's in the morning."

"Claude's family owns that store—what's left of his family," Gerald said. "He lives right by here in an old, old house."

"He doesn't have much to do with family," Catherine said.

Gerald told me then that Claude was supposed to be one of the last genuine living Creoles in New Orleans, a descendant of French aristocrats. He spoke French and Italian and some German, and he was teaching himself Greek so he could read Homer as he was before Alexander Pope had gotten hold of him.

Catherine started to say something but shut her mouth firmly and looked down at her hands.

"Thank you. I feel like—I've been to a celebration," I said, looking at them from the screen door.

Gerald promised to take me to the French Market and show me how to shop there and introduce me to some of his Cajun friends who brought their produce up from places way down on the river. I hadn't known there were any places south of the city, and Gerald said hardly anybody did.

"I've got a little house there, and we'll drive down to see it one day."

"That house," Catherine said. "The walls are full of bees. It's on the verge of becoming a honeycomb."

"I'd better go."

"The door will be open," Gerald said.

On Royal Street, a middle-aged woman with wildly curling hair held up her arm to me so I could see her wristwatch when I asked her the time. "Still time for everything," she said, breathing whiskey fumes at me.

My mother would have long since finished her supper alone in the kitchen and turned on the spotlight in front of the sign that said Bynum's Cabins. In the morning there might be fog, a touch of spring's warm dampness. I shivered.

Someone had kicked away the plank from the stairs. The corridor was lit by a single weak bulb screwed into a ceiling socket. I heard voices, Len's, even and low, my aunt's, loud and resentful. I opened the doors.

Len was standing in front of the hot plate in the tiny kitchen, frying something in a small blackened pan. My aunt, wearing a green satin dressing gown that had seen better days, her feet bare, was sitting on one of the wooden chairs watching him.

"I said you're taking an eternity . . . Jesus! Why are you so slow! You're poky, Len. Do you know what that is? Have you ever thought about it? Fear of life is what it is. You don't take hold. Midwestern fear of life!"

"Aunt Lulu!" I called out.

Her back straightened and she turned her head around to me carefully, as though her neck were stiff. "Helen!" she cried. Plangently, she repeated my name again and again. I stayed close to the doors, abashed. She was holding out her long arms, and the sleeves of her dressing gown fell back. At the fork of the index and middle finger of one hand, so close to the knuckles they appeared to smoke, was the stub of a cigarette. She fell into a fit of violent coughing, and I was saved from having to rush into her arms. Hastily, she brought the stub to her mouth and inhaled. I thought she was strangling. I had the conviction that if I slipped through the doors, back to the corridor, she would forget at once that I'd been there. The coughing ceased. She dropped the stub into a dish near her feet. When she spoke again, her tone was matter-of-fact.

"I'd get up, but I'm feeling a bit frail. Len told me you'd dropped by. I'm sorry I was asleep. I don't—at night anymore. That would be heaven, but such sleep is gone for good. How wonderful to see you! You've grown up. You're a great big pretty girl."

Len waved a fork at me and I waved back as though from a passing trolley.

"I came to New Orleans to see you, Aunt Lulu," I said guard-edly. She still seemed drunk or in some similar state of mental disarray.

"To see me," she said musingly. Then she gestured toward the bed. "Go sit!" she commanded. It had been carelessly made and an ugly pink chenille cover had been thrown across it. Some perversity, or rebellion, made me go and sit on the cot. She didn't seem to notice.

"Now, Beth, is she all right? Not sick or anything?"

"Father died," I said. Len was burning whatever he was frying in the pan. There was a charred smell in the room.

"Oh, pooh! He left home a century ago. Don't tell me Bethie is making a drama out of that! He didn't care about anything except horses anyhow. I warned her about that when she fell for him."

"She isn't happy about it," I said. "I'm not either."

She was smiling. Her teeth were large, tinged with a yellow stain. There was an exaggerated length to her as she sat there with her legs stretched out, the edge of her green robe touch-ing the place where her strong-looking calves began to swell. It was easier for me to see her as a Ziegfeld beauty than my mother.

"I was not speaking of happiness," she said dryly.

I found myself smiling back at her. But I felt sly. I was think-ing of the two sisters cleaning out a cabin together. "Well, really, she sent me down here to ask you to live with her—for a while anyhow."

Aunt Lulu shouted with laughter.

"Do tell! Me live with her! We never got along for more than a minute. That's an old lady's offer. I'm not an old lady yet. I'll write and remind her of a few things *she* may have forgotten—but I haven't."

She narrowed her eyes and stared at me shrewdly. "No, no. Beth knows better. She didn't send you away for that. I never knew a human soul better than I know hers. And I wish I didn't. I dare say she was worried about how it would look—keeping a fully grown daughter by her side forever, like some wicked nineteenth-century female."

"I would have left, if I'd wanted to."

"Would you? I doubt it."

I felt so offended by her jeering, her disparaging words—not so different from my own in my inner and one-sided arguments with Mother—that I rose to my feet. "She speaks so well of you!" I protested.

It was a lie, although Mother could not have spoken about anyone in the way Aunt Lulu had spoken about her. She could not have borne the shock of discovering a malicious sentiment in her own nature.

"Oh-ho! She does, does she!" Aunt Lulu was laughing. "Beth has a way of speaking well of a person that lays them out in funeral garb. Never mind that!" She made a child's wide-eyed movie face, put her finger to her chin. "And I do love Bethie," she crooned in a soppy voice. She paused, peered at me, then added somberly, "As if *that* takes care of the whole show!"

She turned away from me to Len, slapping her hands together. "Isn't that goddamned chop cooked yet? I haven't eaten in days. Helen, hand me my purse. It's underneath the pillow."

I took her the crocodile pocketbook thinking, this is only

Lulu's scene—it doesn't mean anything. That's what Mother
would have said, and she would have smiled with insufferable
understanding and dusted a chair with the corner of her apron.

My aunt was fumbling in the pocketbook, grinding her teeth
with impatience. Finally she came up with a handful of change.
"Len. As soon as you finish with your cooking—Lord, may it
be soon!—go get this girl some beer at Murphy's."

He was walking toward her, carrying the chop on a plate. He
looked at me and shook his head ever so slightly.

"No, thanks," I said quickly. "I don't want anything."

Len put the plate on her lap and she stared down at it intently. "It isn't cut," she said, her mouth pouting. "How can I
cut it on my lap?" Her head fell back against the headpiece of
the chair and she closed her eyes. Slowly, tears welled up beneath her lids and ran down her cheeks. "God!" she gasped.

Len took a small clasp knife from his trouser pocket and cut
the meat. He lifted a piece to her mouth on a fork. "Fee, fie, fo,
fum," she muttered, and opened her mouth to receive the mor-
sel like a bird.

I walked to the tall windows and looked out at the balcony
and then down to the sidewalk on the opposite side of Royal
Street where an elderly man was making his slow way, aided by
a cane. A young fair-haired woman caught up with him. As she
passed him, she suddenly glanced up toward the balcony. It
seemed to me that not only did she see me right through the fil-
igree of the grille, but that our eyes actually met.

"Coffee, Len," my aunt said briskly. "Helen. Come back
here." I returned to the cot. "Let me tell you about myself. It's

been a coon's age since I saw you. New York City, wasn't it? The Astor Hotel?"

"Albany," I corrected her, remembering how she had kept looking at the entrance of that large, nearly empty restaurant, and how sad and empty I'd felt myself in the car with Mother driving home.

"It makes no matter," she said with severity. "I have plans to start a repertory group here. I know it's a sound idea. This ridiculous concentration in the big cities! There's talent everywhere. So much money around now. Look at Claude Maurice de la Fontaine—" she fell silent abruptly and stared at the pieces of meat remaining in the plate on her lap.

"I met him this evening," I said.

She seemed to see me only dimly. Len was staring up at the constellations. I wondered if she was going to pass out. Her gaze sharpened. "Claude. Handsome, isn't he? But not for girls."

"I got a job at Fountain's. That store his family owns. I'm supposed to start work tomorrow."

"You must cultivate him. He'll see that you're promoted in an agreeable, unfair way. You'd think someone like him would want to use his money for art, a cultivated—" She paused and sighed.

She was fading in front of my eyes. She began to move back and forth, feebly, restlessly. "Len tells me you've found a place to live at Gerald Boyd's," she said. She held the plate out to Len. He pushed it very gently back at her. "Please. Finish it," he said. With surprise, I realized those were the first words he had spoken since I'd arrived. What could he have been thinking about all this time?

Lulu seemed to revive. She stamped her foot. "No! I don't want it! Take it away!" she shouted.

Len said nothing but took the plate and returned it to the kitchen. He seemed so accustomed to it all. He lit a cigarette and went to perch on the edge of the bed.

"Gerald will see to you. And Catherine. Gerald takes care of everyone—or imagines he does. It's not possible to do, you know, take care of anyone. But there are these living saints. Not a saint, our Claude. A fallen angel."

We sat silently for a while. Lulu sighed now and then. Len clasped his hands and bent his head. It was like waiting in a hospital or a bus station.

"Claude is living on the brink," she said at last. "He's been a foolish boy. The bogeyman is out to get him."

"You don't know that," Len said flatly.

"Oh yes I do!" she retorted. "Not a leaf falls but that I hear about it! Howard Meade hears everything, and being the malicious old harridan he is, he tells me all!"

"Why do you pass it around? All this vague—"

"It's not vague. All I suggested was that Claude is in trouble. People with his inclination are always in trouble."

"Everybody's in trouble," Len said. He smiled faintly. "That's life!"

"What's life?" my aunt asked in a singsong voice.

"A magazine."

"How much?"

"A nickel."

"I haven't got a nickel."

"That's life!" said Len.

They laughed and looked at me expectantly. I tried to smile. The silliness of their routine—had she taught it to him?—the playfulness of it, seemed the greatest evidence I'd seen of their being lovers. How squalid! How perfectly awful I felt, discarded, out of everything, with no reason for being anywhere.

"What about that coffee?" my aunt asked.

"If you want," he said.

"Oh, never mind." She sat up straight and cleared her throat and looked at me soberly. "Of course, you know I can't go to Beth. It's a fairy tale of hers, that she and I are close. We never have been. You simply wouldn't have dreamed that such a plump, pretty little woman was capable of such outrageous fancies. She's tried to live them, too—like seeing herself married to a rich man with a string of racehorses. I quite liked your father. He was a rather simple fellow, really, who had room in his heart for only one passion, maybe one and a half passions. And he wasn't rich!"

But Aunt Lulu had invented an infant, Len had told me, its life and its death! Were people utterly unknown to themselves?

"He wanted her when he saw her up there on the stage," my aunt said in a muted voice, remembering. "She was a lovely thing. Not like noisy old me."

I shivered, sensing for an instant the implacable forces of time and loss. Aunt Lulu was more alert than I had imagined. "Cold?" she asked, with a touch of irony. I shook my head, embarrassed and irritated.

"I suppose you are real to her," she said. "I'm certainly not."

She held out her hands, palms upward, and shrugged. "There's no place to go once you land here," she said with an air of exhaustion, as though she were only now at the final stop of a long journey. "This is the end of the country—not the delta, not those vile little settlements in that hellish swamp Gerald is so crazy about even though some bastards who live there nearly killed him."

She stared at me, watching, waiting.

"What are you talking about?" I asked, weary of her mystifications. She smiled, gratified.

"This is a dangerous country, all of it. I've been on the road. I know."

"You shouldn't tell her private things about people. It's not right," Len said indignantly.

"Oh, hush! What a little prig you are!" she exclaimed, frowning at him. "She should know. She's going to be living with them."

"They told me about his wife," I said quickly.

"No . . . that's not what I'm talking about. It's what those savages in the bayou did to him. He won a prize for his poetry, a big, sophisticated city prize, and of course the local newspaper wrote him up. Those bayou creatures got wind of it, word of mouth, I suppose, since I don't believe for a second that they can read! The poems were about them. About their lives. Beautiful poems. And they took offense. What right did he have to write poems about *them*. They grabbed him one night. They held him on the ground and stuck a hose into his poor bottom and blew air up him." She paused and observed me, studied my face as if to measure the horror she must have seen on it.

"I hate that story," Len said fiercely.

"He had a heart attack after that, because of what they did to him," Aunt Lulu went on imperturbably. "His country-folk friends. He wouldn't tell the police who did it to him. Howard says he still sees them."

"The same ones?" I asked with a histrionic disbelief that was really an effort to ward off the vision of Gerald Boyd, helpless, his face pressed into the earth.

"Knowing him, I wouldn't be surprised," she said. She stood up and swayed. "Help me," she said piteously to Len. He took her arm and led her to the bed. "I'm so tired," she said. "But, Helen, we'll see a good deal of each other."

She fell upon the bed; her hands bunched up the chenille cover and she rested her cheek on it. The robe slowly slipped from her legs. The bottoms of her feet were gray.

"Helen? Did you see the constellations up there on the ceiling?" Her voice issued from the cover with renewed force. "Do the stars make you feel small? Do human concerns seem insignificant to you when you gaze up at them? Not me." She lifted her head with effort and rolled her eyes at me. She meant, I supposed, to be comic, but she wasn't. She only looked sick and weak. "No!" she pronounced with ferocity, as though she'd sensed pity and hated it. "The stars make me feel huge—as if I could eat them all up."

I glanced up involuntarily at those constellations painted probably over one hundred years ago. I was afraid of them, of the past, of what I had heard that evening. When I looked back at Aunt Lulu, she appeared to sleep. As he had done earlier on this long day, Len motioned me toward the great doors.

"She looks so ill," I said to him in the corridor. "I wish she hadn't told me those things about Gerald Boyd, and Claude."

"She is ill," he said. "And she shouldn't have done, shouldn't have passed on such gossip."

"Is it gossip?"

"I don't know. Some of it perhaps."

"I forgot how you met her?"

"In a bar," he answered. We went down the stairs and stood at the threshold of the courtyard. It was faintly illuminated by a lamp in one of the tall windows that looked down upon it. When Len said "in a bar," I recalled what he had told me earlier, that he had gone to Lulu to get a job.

"I was having a drink with Howard Meade," he was saying. "He owns the bookstore where I worked a few weeks when I first came to the city. He knew Lulu. I didn't know much about drinking—how that can be the only reason people know each other. She and Howard don't speak if they meet on the street when they're both sober. Well, she was in the bar. She'd torn her dress somehow and was clutching it and she fell over a stool and began to moan in the most awful way, like an animal. Howard was on the point of passing out. I brought her home. I thought she was going to die. But she wouldn't let me get help. She was coming off a week's bender. She was only just able to tell me what to do to help her."

"You said you'd gone to her looking for work," I said in a frozen voice.

Len walked into the courtyard and stood with his back to me.

"So I did," he said mildly, turning to face me. "I took her home because she couldn't have made it alone. And I came back to see her a few days later because I had seen one of her posters for her repertory theater. She didn't remember the night in the bar, my washing her and putting her to bed. I didn't remind her. I didn't know then that that night wasn't exceptional."

How mean-spirited I was! It occurred to me that I had a suspicious nature, something I'd not realized until that moment. To apologize seemed too intimate an act, but I wanted to, even though I hadn't said, right out, that I thought he'd lied to me.

"You've been very good to her," I said. He didn't see my effort to smile gratefully; he was sitting down on the rim of the fountain. Above him, the marble girl reached out with her arboreal limbs. He beckoned to me and I went, gladly, to sit down beside him. It seemed a very private place, though someone pausing at a window and looking down could have seen us. Above, in the square of sky formed by the edges of the roof, real stars glimmered. But the sky had a varnished look, as though the painter of Aunt Lulu's ceiling had had a hand in it, too.

"I didn't meet her so long ago, only two months or so," Len said, speaking in a low voice and glancing up at the windows from time to time. "It seems a lot longer. I'd never taken care of anyone before, not even a dog. When I went to college in Chicago, I hardly spoke to people. I can see myself walking across the campus, hurrying from one class to another, afraid someone might say something to me, want something."

He stared at me steadily, wonderingly, for a long moment as though I might explain to him why he had been like that.

"Well, you were only a boy . . ."

He shook his head. "I couldn't climb up out of myself," he said. "If someone said hello, it was like an explosion."

"Why did you quit working in the bookstore? It sounds better than waiting on tables."

"Howard Meade was erratic with money. You have to be independently wealthy to be his employee. If I asked for my pay when he was sober, he'd give it to me, very Old South, full of courtly apologies that I'd even had to ask for it. When he was drunk, which he was most of the time, he'd curse me or else not appear on payday. Even sober, he has a cold indignation about everything under the sun. And he takes a kind of cold joy in confounding people with all he knows about books, even his customers."

There was a dark tea-colored stain on the arch of one of the marble girl's feet. "Her hands are turning into branches."

"It's Daphne," he told me as if I'd asked him the name of a girl at a party. "She escaped from Apollo by turning into a tree."

He smoked a cigarette. It was tranquil there in the courtyard, domestic and hidden and almost intimate.

"Is that true? About what happened to Gerald Boyd?"

"I believe so. I've heard nearly the same story from other people."

I wanted to know whomever he knew. It seemed extraordinary that Gerald could cook, read a magazine, write his poems, do anything in ordinary life. It was the way I'd felt about a woman my mother had known whose house had burned down with her husband and younger child inside it. A year later, I had seen her planting seedlings in a plot in front of her new house, her surviving son kneeling beside her, a trowel in his small hands.

"Then—anything can happen."

"Yes. Anything."

"When I met Claude de la Fontaine tonight, I made such a foolish mistake." I told Len about the book, how I'd thought it was about Adolph Hitler. "I've heard him on the radio. It's like listening to a dog fight," I said.

"If you understood German, you'd hear what a nightmare he is."

"Do you?"

"A little. My mother speaks it. I took it in college, but dropped it. Then after two years, I dropped college, too."

His family had been terribly distressed, he said, but polite in the way they expressed their disappointment. "That was nearly the worst of it—that wounded politeness."

His brother was a mathematician, and his sister, a flutist, was going to music school. He hadn't been able to *go* to his own life, he said, the way they had. But how could you plan a life with everything that was happening in the world? He'd be drafted any day. He had come to New Orleans last February, to "see the Mardi Gras." He smiled. "It was as good a reason as any."

"How was it?"

"Wonderful music. And people going crazy, wearing wild clothes, drunk, dancing. I stayed on because I like it here—the way people behave as if they'd known you forever."

He had gripped the rim of the fountain with his hands and was leaning over, his shoulders slightly hunched. I could imagine him walking about the college campus. Seeing the thinness of his body, I felt an intense, nearly unbearable pity that pierced me to my bones. There was a faint smell of burnt lamb about him from cooking Lulu's supper, mixed with a fresh, bland smell of some plain soap.

About Matthew there had always lingered a whiff of solvent from his tweed jackets that he had dry-cleaned too often.

I wanted to sleep for days. Tomorrow, I had to go to work, to sell undergarments to southern women.

"You have to hear them play 'When the Saints Go Marching In,'" he told me.

"Them?"

"The Negroes. On the way to a funeral, they play a dirge, but after the funeral, they play 'The Saints' . . . It makes you mad with joy."

"I must go back to my room." My heart beat thickly, heavily. But he did not say, "Not yet, not yet!" "Tomorrow is my first day at work," I explained, though no explanation had been asked for. I bent to pick up my pocketbook. A corner of the prisoner's letter stuck up out of it. I showed it to Len, telling him where I'd found it.

He reached into his shirt pocket and took out a stamp, its edges curled. "This was for a letter home that I know I won't write," he said. "Give me that. I'll mail it for you."

He walked with me down Royal Street. He was such a sub-dued man, not exactly sad but with something lonesome and adrift about him. What would he be like—mad with joy? Did he make love to my aunt? I felt the movement of his walking. His arm brushed against mine. I wanted to look at him. I didn't dare for fear he would read in my face what was in my mind.

I said that my mother and Lulu were utterly unalike. "It's

hard for me to believe they are sisters." There was a tremor in my voice. What had I said? Something about my mother and Lulu? Or had I said I could see his silver head resting on my aunt's breasts?

"My father is a rabbi," he said suddenly as we came to St. Phillip.

I halted, astonished. "But I thought priests couldn't marry!"

He burst into laughter. "Helen, my father is often priestly, but he's no priest."

He touched my hand with a direct friendliness he hadn't shown me before. And he had called me by my name. "Shall I explain?"

"No . . . not yet. This day has flustered me so." *Flustered* was a word my mother would have used. "*Adolphe* and now rabbis," I said. I tried to smile because he was smiling. "I seem to have forgotten everything I knew. What little that is . . ."

"Don't be embarrassed," he said. "Just have good luck to-morrow."

As I walked toward Gerald's house, I turned back involuntarily. Len was gone.

People steal into one's consciousness and occupy what seems, in retrospect, to have been their place all along.

I had met most of the people who were to figure in my life for the next few months and long after I left New Orleans, but not one of the most consequential, a girl named Nina Weir.

Actually, I had already seen her through the wrought-iron grille of the balcony outside the ballroom when she looked up from Royal Street, sensing, perhaps, a presence at the window, staring down at her.

CHAPTER

FIVE

One early evening, a week or so after I had met him at Gerald Boyd's, I glimpsed Claude de la Fontaine crossing St. Louis Square toward the Cabildo. For a moment he paused, and I could see him clearly in his white linen suit. Light from one of the tall lamps that stood about the square illuminated his wide forehead and made hollows of his eyes. He was motionless; he looked like a statue out of antiquity. Then a young man with black hair and a thin curved nose like the beak of a small bird emerged from Pirates Alley and went swiftly to him.

They spoke a word or two. When Claude glanced quickly around, I shrank back behind a long bench. Claude, placing a hand on the young man's buttocks, pressed him against himself until he was resting his whole slender length against Claude as a sleepy child rests against his father. A second later, they vanished down the alley.

A knowledge I didn't want entered me stealthily. My aunt had made it clear that women held no attraction for Claude. But there is a difference between knowing and seeing.

I had learned a few things about ladies' underwear that week, and something of the ferocity of women in mortal fear of the aging of their bodies who, before trying one on, seized corsets almost angrily and stretched them as far as they could, tweaked hooks and eyes, pinched the elastic facings and panels and yanked at the garters so violently I was afraid they'd tear them off. If the corset passed this first test, a woman would go grimly into a dressing room to see how much of herself could be contained and flattened by what I came to think of as pink armor of the deep—there was something both organic and aquatic to me about those garments. Young girls bought slips and underpants quickly, often without trying them on. On their breasts and bottoms, silk and cotton cloth rested lightly. A salesgirl in ladies' dresses told me it was a great deal easier to sell underwear because the customers had secret, unshakable convictions about what they must have. But with dresses, you had to convince, to sell.

It was not hard work for me. I saw boredom up ahead like a crater in the road, but the job would do for now. It took so little attention—I learned the stock soon enough—that I could muse about my real life in the Quarter, the life my wages made possible.

I had eaten supper several times with Gerald and Catherine. When I got home, I had found a place set for me. It was lovely to be so welcomed, and I felt awkward about it. "You're spending all the money I pay you for rent on feeding me," I said to

Catherine. "Soon, I'll eat more, and then more, and you'll have to take in another boarder just to be able to afford me." She said for me not to worry for a while. They were pleased to have me there at the supper table, and after I got settled, in another week or two, we could work something out. At supper that night, Gerald said I was welcome, he liked to cook, I was so appreciative, and later on, maybe I'd fix them some northern meals. He'd heard about that food up there, beans and maple syrup, wasn't it?

The gentle pleasantries were interrupted by the appearance at the screen door of a round-faced man with eyeglasses, grinning. Just behind him, I saw a small plump figure swathed in a brilliant vermillion stole. "That's Norman Lindner and his wife, Marlene," Catherine said to me. "He's from the north, too," Gerald said. When the Lindners were standing in the room, Catherine whispered to me that he was a painter.

"It was unanimous," Lindner said to Gerald triumphantly.

"Say hello first, Norm," said his wife. She was looking at me in an inventorial way. I had the feeling she wanted me to stand up so she could see what kind of shoes I had on. She wore heavy makeup and high-heeled pumps. At the corner of each eye, she had drawn a thick black mark as though to make herself look Oriental.

Norman Lindner said hello to Catherine and nodded in my direction. "You hear about that, Gerald? Unanimous! Charles Evans Hughes is the light of this nation!"

"Sit down a while," Gerald said mildly. "You'll wear yourself out with joy. This is our friend, Helen Bynum, who's renting the room over the kitchen. She's from up north, too."

"Hello, Helen," Lindner said, looking at me for a second,

then back at Gerald. "What do you say, Gerry? If the whole Supreme Court is agreed about this decision, don't you see which way the wind is blowing?"

"I say Hughes may be the light of the nation. But the wind blows from all over the place. You can't make white people think kindly about colored people traveling first-class, if they do travel first-class. Sit down, Marlene, why don't you. We'll have coffee."

"We can't stay. We're going to see some paintings by a friend of mine. Kindly thoughts aren't the issue. Thoughts change anyhow, but they'll never change without fair laws."

"Are you an artist, Helen?" Marlene asked in a high fluting voice.

"I work at Fountain's," I replied. "I sell ladies' underwear."

"Oh, my!" Marlene exclaimed.

"We have to go. Anyhow, Gerry old dear, it's a great day for the Constitution."

After they had left, Catherine said she wished Norman wouldn't call Gerald *Gerry*. "It makes me feel like keeling over."

"I don't mind," Gerald said. "He wants everything to be familiar."

Catherine smoked a cigarette, one elbow on the table supporting her cheek. "He's an irritating man, and he knows it. When he pushes you as far as he can, he starts to ask your advice to, you know, soften you up. He's strange."

"We all are," Gerald said.

"He's stranger. He sees plots. He thinks he's being overheard constantly by powerful people who are gathering damning evidence against him."

She spoke with unusual severity. She laughed suddenly. Gerald smiled at her and reached over and patted her head. "Now don't pat me like that," she protested sweetly. "Norman is truly as boring as sawdust and you know it. He wants life to be like those WPA murals he painted—big meaty working stiffs marching as to war against the bosses. Imbeciles of virtue."

"He just craves order," Gerald said. "He doesn't want people all mixed up and contrary. He really loves villains, they save wear and tear on the brain."

There was a suggestion of a practiced scene between them. I thought of Mother trying with all her graces to soften my hard heart. That had been a scene, not altogether false but not quite true either. It struck me that Gerald, with his apparently limitless availability and equally limitless tolerance, overheard people, too. And he must come to private inner judgments.

He was always ready to listen to and talk with those who came through the screeen door of an evening, and for all I knew, the whole day long. There had been others besides the Lindners who had stopped by that week and whom I'd glimpsed in the garden on my way to my room. Once, a man had called to Gerald from the street and he had left the table and not returned until Catherine and I had finished supper.

She had told me a little about her family, her father, whose mother had been a Blackfoot Indian, a brother who had died young of meningitis. But I could tell she was listening for Gerald, wanting him to come back to us. When we heard his slow footsteps, she murmured to me, "People don't understand how careful he's supposed to be—and he can't be. They eat him up and he wants to be eaten up."

A couple of weekends later, I met my Aunt Lulu's former

husband, Dr. Samuel Bridge, who came to supper with Claude de la Fontaine to eat Gerald's famous jambalaya. On that Saturday, Gerald had taken me to the French Market, and I met two of his Cajun friends from down the river who held out to him handfuls of living crabs, green and gray like stones, and wet and moving frantically. He was a different man with them, excited, a little quarrelsome yet rollicking and affectionate, speaking with an accent close to theirs.

I quailed at the thought that these men might be the very same men who had done the terrible thing to him. I stood apart, wishing I hadn't come. Bearing sacks of food—including the crabs, which moved ceaselessly at the bottom of the sacks—he took me to the same café near the market where I had had my first cup of New Orleans coffee.

"You persuade Lulu yet to go up north?" he asked me as we drank our coffee.

I clapped my hand to my forehead. He laughed. The marble counter was cool beneath my sweaty fingers as I brushed at crumbs from my beignet.

"Maybe this is the best place for her," he said.

"I don't see how she can go on with that drinking."

"They live a long time sometimes," he said vaguely.

"Len ought to move in with her," I suggested tentatively.

"Oh, no," he protested. "He ain't made up his mind about anything yet."

"He could take care of her better that way," I said lamely.

Gerald said nothing to that. I couldn't get out of him what I wanted, the truth about Len and my aunt. I changed the subject and told him I'd written to my mother and told her enough about my aunt's condition for her to fill in the rest. I had thought there'd be a crisis, even imagining my mother arriving in New Orleans to shanghai her sister and transport her to the stern dry confines of the old house. But she wrote back that everything was fine, she'd found a "stout country girl" who was working out better than she had any reason to expect, that business was good. Too bad about Lulu, she wrote, but she expected it was just a stage, part of what women had to go through when they were getting too old for certain things. She didn't name the things.

The drama of my coming south to fetch the sister of the bereaved widow had faded away, a rootless idea. It was I who worried about Lulu. I'd been in New Orleans over a month. I tried not to, but couldn't help thinking about the days she was alone, drunk in the ballroom, staggering down the stairs and across the stream to go out and buy the po'boy sandwiches I guessed she lived on when Len wasn't around to bring her food.

Gerald made the jambalaya in the kitchen. I could see him through a crack in the wide floorboards of my little room. He looked up at the crack now and then, a knife in his hand for chopping vegetables, and used a Cajun accent to tell me how he was cooking the stew. But then he was a poet, and it didn't mean he was mocking anyone; just a bit more distant from his own life than other people are.

I had a copy of his volume of poems that Catherine had given me. In school, I had read Milton and Thomas Gray and Wordsworth and Longfellow and Edwin Markham, and Joyce Kilmer, whom I had hated because of having to memorize "Trees." Gerald's poems were not like any I had read. They didn't rhyme; they were short, eight or ten lines. They were like small explosions in bare rooms, and the last lines had a kind of delayed effect on me, the way you suddenly see something you thought you'd understood forever, in an entirely different way. Here and there were words I didn't know, almost French, like the ones the Cajun men in the market had used. There was a grief-stricken quality about the poems, not an elaborate, theatrical grief, but one that was simple, pure, inconsolable.

The two guests arrived within a few minutes of each other that evening. Dr. Bridge came first. He was thin, not tall, with a rather long face. He took off his eyeglasses when he ate and then he looked much younger. In his agreeable husky voice, he said to me, "I'm almost your uncle."

He was holding my hand lightly. I felt mortified as though I was obliged to account for my debauched relative. He let go of my hand. "I'm only sorry I'm not," he said. Could he possibly still want to be married to her?

He had turned from me and was speaking to Catherine. His uniform fit him perfectly, as though he had had it made by his own tailor. His brown hair was more crinkled than curly.

Had he meant to compliment me by saying he regretted he was not my uncle? The core of the compliment—if that's what it was—eluded me. Gerald had told me, "Sam's a ladies' man." Perhaps a ladies' man could not resist inviting everyone to himself. I stared at Dr. Bridge as he stood so gracefully beside Catherine. Everything visible about him had a cool and extreme tidiness, one, I imagined, that could arouse a wish to see him, or make him, disheveled, self-forgetful. I thought then that Gerald had been wrong when he said that Dr. Bridge was worried about Aunt Lulu, and that Catherine was closer to the truth. He visited her to assure himself of her wish to see him. I thought of the beefily handsome man who had accompanied his wife to the underwear department at the store last week and had said, not looking at me, that the management had picked the right representative to sell these beautiful scraps of things to women. His wife, who required more than a scrap of a thing to go around her middle, gave him a dark sad look while he smiled up heartlessly at a ceiling light. I shuddered for Lulu in all her helpless disorder.

Although I had seen Claude briefly before, when he opened the screen door and walked into the room, it was as if I were seeing him for the first time. He had a kind of beauty I had thought of as existing largely in nature, unhuman, in noble trees, serene, unpeopled landscapes, in certain animals, horses, cats.

I sat across the table from him and I heard less of the conversation than I might have if I could have stopped looking at him. In any event, the four of them were all old friends and much of what they said referred to people and events I had no knowledge of. Mostly, I felt a childish pleasure like that of listening to grown-ups without, myself, being obliged to speak and interrupt my musing about them.

Claude mentioned a magazine that was doing a feature story on artists in the French Quarter which would include Gerald and Norman Lindner, the painter.

"That's the new thing, isn't it?" Gerald said. "Now you've got to see faces. Nobody more is going to read my poems than already have."

"Norman will like it," Claude said in his soft deep voice. "He'll become real to himself at last."

"He's already too real to himself," Catherine said.

"You're right!" Claude said. Catherine smiled with a certain shyness and touched Claude's sleeve briefly. I felt a twinge of jealousy. I didn't know about what or whom. They began to speak of a novel by a Negro writer, Richard Wright, that had been published the year before. I had not heard of it; I had never heard of any Negro writer.

"He doesn't understand white people," Gerald said.

"Who does?" Claude remarked lightly. "And why should he? What about Countee Cullen? And Jean Toomer? Do they?"

"They don't write about white people," said Gerald.

"Which white people?" asked Claude. "You sound like you're speaking of a gelatinous mass."

"That's what I mean. How can we seem otherwise to colored people? My neighbor Julius, who comes out to sit in his chair and talk with me in the afternoon from time to time, I asked him if he read it, and he says Wright doesn't know anything about colored people either."

"Who's Julius?" I asked Catherine in an undertone.

"He lives down the street where the colored section starts. He's about eighty, but you'd never guess it—it's the way dark-skinned people don't show age." She raised her voice and said to everyone at the table, "But he's so old, Gerald. He wouldn't like it that such a young man wrote a book anyhow. And to show all that murdering. It would upset Julius. He's kind of an old prig."

"Why, Catherine!" Dr. Bridge exclaimed, smiling. "You mean to say your colored friend thinks Wright was being uppity?"

"Julius got hold of something," Gerald said. "That lawyer, Max—you-all believe in communist saints? Bigger's got to die—and he tells him to die free. Poor Bigger's getting killed by words as well as by the state. And that lawyer tells him about buildings and how they're held up by people like him. Speaking with God's voice."

"But it's a wonderful book," Claude said then. "You have to think about it and read it again, and read parts of it over and over until it begins to overcome you and you see what Wright has done. It's the state that *is* Kurtz—Kurtz in *The Heart of Darkness*—that's what Wright shows. When Max says about Bigger: 'His very existence is a crime against the state!' Wright's telling you everything. Max is all sentimental virtue—nearly unbearable. It doesn't matter. Social virtue is the hardest for a writer. What are you going to say about *Everyman*, Gerald? That it's full of stock characters? You've missed something. The novel is about passion. It's like a fire."

"That's good, Claude. Really good," Gerald said.

"You have outdone yourself with this jambalaya," Dr. Bridge said. "You get tired of poetry, Gerald, and you can open a restaurant in the Quarter."

"You trying to change the subject, Sam?" asked Claude.

"Just the object," Dr. Bridge replied. "This young lady from the north will think we don't talk about anything but colored folk."

"We were speaking of tribes," Claude said. "In one way or another, it's what people mostly talk about."

"And food," said Dr. Bridge.

"And food," Claude repeated, smiling at him.

"And love," Dr. Bridge added.

For an instant, I was nearly overcome with panic. I saw myself running out of the room, into the street, finding there was no more air to breathe there, either. But I felt, too, exhilaration at the thought of what I had escaped when I stepped from the train into this country of shock. I drew a great breath of air—it had come back—and Claude glanced at me.

"It's humidity," he said. "You might get used to it."

I smiled. Was there solicitude in his face? Would I get used to everything, finally, understand it? Would it be possible for someone like Claude to conceive of the world I had come from, one I saw as gray, frozen, where I would have become like my mother, my mouth working with mindless sayings to quell the terror in my heart—or else I might have ended up, had I stayed, like the naked old woman who had been found one spring roaming the meadows above Rhinebeck in a torrent of rain, howling like a wolf.

The remains of the pungent stew lay on my plate like relics gathered from the bottom of the sea. They were speaking quietly in their southern voices, finishing their suppers, every scrap, like good children. I would have to learn to eat differently.

Later, when I was sitting on the rim of the fountain, Claude came to sit beside me. The other three were in the kitchen, talking, laughing now and then. Dr. Bridge and Catherine were leaning against the wall, smoking cigarettes while Gerald made coffee.

"I think I work for you," I said to Claude.

"Gerald told me. Are they good to you in the store?"

"Very good. People are friendly. I'm selling underwear, but I've been told I'll get to sell suits one of these days." I heard in my voice a touch of self-mockery. He might not appreciate that. "That'll be more interesting," I said quickly.

"It could be like making up a story," he said. "You'll tell a nice story about the suit, how dazzling it will be on a lady. Then she'll want it."

"But the drinking fountains . . . I've never seen that. Little signs on each, one that says Colored, the other White."

He spoke as though he hadn't heard what I'd said.

"Actually, I don't have much to do with the store. I do get money from it and I'm obliged to attend meetings now and then. Others run it. I shouldn't be any good at that at all. I'm too scatterbrained."

I had not expected him to be disingenuous.

"People have a horror of those they've mistreated," he went on. "There'll be one big fountain one of these days. We'll certainly be in this war, you know, and Negroes will fight in it. Of course, no one will like that great big fountain where everyone can drink. People will be angry for a century, the abusers and the abused. But the law will change. It can't hold back what's been held back since slavery days."

He had heard me about the drinking fountains. Perhaps he was someone who didn't try to answer everything right away. He lit a cigarette. His left hand rested on his knees. He wore a small gold ring with a reddish stone in it.

"What a beautiful ring," I remarked, thinking of his hand, his strong-looking fingers and ivory skin. He slipped it off at once and held it out. I leaned forward into the light from the kitchen. I could see a carved face in the stone.

"Hermes," he said. "It's a carnelian. A gift long ago."

I had loved Uncle Morgan. I couldn't feel that love now, but it was there when I recalled my childhood, my father. Uncle Morgan had brought a kind of world radiance into our house. He had made my father laugh as I never heard him laugh in anyone else's presence.

We sat silently for a little while, listening to the agreeable murmur from the kitchen. Claude didn't smell of lemons this evening but of something else. Weeks later, when I was in his house, I saw on a chest of drawers a cut-glass bottle of Guerlain cologne.

"There's something left out of Saxons, of northern people," he said softly, as though telling a secret. "I think they never got used to the fact that there are openings in the human body. That may account for why they are so much given to massacres and slaughter without even the excuse of religious faith. Though they've murdered for that, too, like the rest of the world. Mediterraneans are different."

I was utterly disconcerted. No one had ever spoken to me in such a fashion. But almost I wanted to laugh aloud the way my father had laughed in his brother's presence, without constraint.

"Saxons don't, I imagine, see themselves that way," I said.

"Oh, that! I don't believe people can look at themselves very clearly, do you? No one is free enough. How do you leap out of your own nature and look down at it? Laws may be the nearest human beings get to self-criticism."

"What really happened to Gerald?" I asked in a whisper. He glanced quickly toward the kitchen as if I were alluding to something of the moment. I thought—Gerald is a person who is now always in danger. "I meant the beating," I added.

"I think on some days that I understand what happened. Then I don't at all. A great deal was made of him for a while, after the prize. He is a native son—all that."

"I've read his poems. I don't see how they could have given such offense. I would have thought those people he wrote about—though from the poems I wouldn't have known he was writing about any special people if my aunt hadn't told me—I should think *they* would have given him a prize."

"He made their lives his subject. He marked them out and made them seem different to themselves. Perhaps he made them aware they had selves."

"Don't people want to be distinguished? That is, different?"

"No," he replied, smiling faintly. "I should say," he amended, "that *some* people don't want to be different. For them, to be noticed at all is to become monstrous, disgusting."

"But what they did to him—" I paused. My voice died away. I saw it. Night. Gerald struggling on the ground, held down by thick hands. His clothes torn off.

"It wasn't planned, I think. They saw him taking a stroll one evening, perhaps toward one of the little piers on the river in some little settlement down there on the delta. He never said which. And three of them set upon him."

"But they had a *hose*! I mean—there are steps, plans, that lead to such a thing . . ."

"They had a length of hose . . . probably lying on the ground in someone's yard. The most ordinary thing."

"And he's still friends with them, still goes down there."

Catherine paused by the kitchen door. "Coffee is coming," she called to us.

"That's because he really understands them. That is why the poems have such tenderness," Claude said, leaning toward me very slightly. "He knows what they're capable of, yet he has enormous sympathy. How can sympathy be anything but cheap sentiment if you don't know the dark side?"

"But they worked out the dark side on his own body!"

The three came out of the kitchen at that moment, Dr. Bridge and Catherine carrying coffee cups. The light behind them darkened their figures as they moved slowly toward us. They looked like figures in a dream. All at once I smelled coffee, felt the warm damp air, heard the rustle of Catherine's skirt. It was as if my senses had slept, all except hearing, while Claude was trying to explain what couldn't be explained.

Sam Bridge was smiling at me as he held out a cup. Everything had meaning for me, the sharp line of his pressed cuff, Gerald's hair catching the light, which also touched my sandals and the weave of the linen of Claude's trouser legs, Catherine's shy, sweet laugh about something Gerald had bent forward to say into her ear.

As I went to bed that night, pulling back the almost weight-less cover, I thought about how respectful and attentive Claude was with Gerald and Catherine. Later, I came to see that he was particularly that way with anyone in whom he sensed suffering, as though he were ineluctably drawn to what repelled most people.

CHAPTER

SIX

When I stopped by the ballroom in the evening or on a Sunday, I occasionally brought my aunt food in a pie dish covered with a handkerchief, leftovers from one of Gerald's suppers or else from something I had cooked for myself. Even before greeting her, I would go to the minuscule kitchen and transfer the contents of the dish to one of the three chipped blue-and-white plates, and I would not refer to it in whatever conversation followed. When she was asleep—or passed out—I came and went, a food-bearing shadow. Later, she would eat a little of what I'd brought. I learned this from Len, who also told me she felt chagrined by my bringing her food—especially when she awoke and found it there. But she did eat it. I didn't know what to do, so I kept on bringing it. My concern for her was often resentful, probably because there was so little affection in it.

In my mother's infrequent letters there was never a hint that she would like me to come home. It seemed she had been as freed from the monotony of our life together by my departure as I had been, or else there was a studied effort on her part to suggest that was so. She'd gone to the doctor when a cold persisted, and he'd told her she had the heart and blood pressure of a young woman. She often resorted to capitals to convey emotion. It looked childish, but it was effective; I could hear her voice rise in triumph over that "young woman."

Matthew wrote once. His penmanship was so lacking in temperament that after a quick glance, I folded up the single sheet of paper and dropped it on a chair. I decided I would not read it; his handwriting was an affront in itself. A few minutes later, feeling foolish, I picked it up. There was nothing in the contents that diverged from the look of the letter. I wondered that we'd ever lain together on an old musty mattress, naked and gasping, in the attic where he took me out of respect for his mother who, in any case, was stone deaf.

I no longer believed Len was Lulu's lover. There might have been something between them once, but now, even though he continued to do errands for her or tried to ease her, change her moods when she was irritable, wipe the sweat from her face when she was sick, I saw how he looked as if he were in a trance of boredom when he was there. I felt a vagrant hope because he was, in a sense, turning away from her toward me. If we met in the ballroom, he always walked home with me when I left. Now and then we drank beers at Murphy's bar.

We were odd together. He was both remote and confiding as he sat across from me in the dark booth. I was, once we were alone, tense with the effort to restrain my feeling for him. We were united but imprisoned by our different ties to Lulu. We spoke of her as though we were two actors in a movie, dressed like doctors and carrying toy stethoscopes.

Even if she was chagrined by my bringing her food, my aunt appeared glad to see me, a tremulous, frail gladness that I suspected was partly an act. But I was relieved that she no longer greeted me in the noisy rough way she had when I first began to see her more or less regularly. When she was sober enough, she would talk about her family, our family. Then the weight of duty slipped from my shoulders, and I didn't mark the passing hours.

"Your grandfather was a hardhearted man," she told me. "He was smart though, and disdainful because of it. When our mother died, he let his heart turn to stone. Of course, I know he was shocked by both his daughters becoming chorus girls. What he wanted was learned children, detached, book-reading girls with modest hairstyles and cool virginal voices." She laughed. "That ought to teach you not to expect what you want from your children. Well—he was fair in his stony way. I'll say that for him. I dare say he was horribly lonely. But he was one of those people, those men, whose loneliness confirms their general pessimism—so, in an odd way, it made him smug. Of course, your mother would never say such things about him. As far as she was concerned, he was a tragic figure. And brilliant. Naturally. We used to fight about that. It was pointless except the fights gave her a chance to boast about her loyalty. I can't think why she and I are so different! How busy she always was showing herself her own virtues—patience, cheerful stoicism, understanding . . ." She broke off and stared up at the starred ceiling. Her hands gripped each other. "She understood *nothing*," she muttered.

"She'd never say a word against my father," I said.

"Oh, no!" she exclaimed, lowering her head and looking at me. "It would have reflected on her. She was enormously vain." She smiled as if Mother's vanity were an endearing trait. "But that nearly stumped her. Could she have said he was right to leave her? Hardly. And she did suffer. She couldn't find a way of making it right—and preserve herself. It nearly broke her. That might have been a good thing, though. If she had broken—just once."

Aunt Lulu sighed deeply. "I think I've made up for my sister's making a virtue out of every weakness—I've managed to do the exact opposite. When I became an actress, I was tortured by the fear of criticism because I knew it would be true. But even if Beth hadn't married your father, I don't believe she would have become an actress. She would have dreaded criticism, too, as I did. But for a different reason. She would have feared the critics were too stupid to see how wonderful she was!"

I started to laugh, and at once my laughter sounded too loud, a touch false in my own ears. Lulu was laughing, too, but not, I felt, from the discordant union of guilt and pleasure that our conversations about Mother roused up in me.

"Did you know Uncle Morgan?"

She looked puzzled. "Of course I did. Didn't Bethie tell you? I was half gone on him."

She must have seen how startled I was. She laughed rather

coarsely. "I warn you! If you think you've got things straight in your mind, give it up! He was so appealing . . . he was all gaiety, sweetness. And it wasn't at all clear, at least not to me, that he was more taken with men. I say *more* because there was a certain ambiguity about him—well, I was used to tiny chorus boys like dolls their mothers had made out of bird bones and feather and bits of panne and silk."

"I only remember a kind of atmosphere he brought with him," I said. "Was he like Claude de la Fontaine?"

"Claude's like a lioness." She smiled a little. "Your Uncle Morgan was not as female."

"What did my mother think?"

"Why, she said Morgan was the greatest catch in the eastern part of the United States!"

"She couldn't have not known—something."

"People can *not* know anything they want to. Do you really believe people understand each other?" She paused and shook her head. "They can't," she said.

"I don't believe that," I said.

"Oh—you can give names to things . . . Really, I'm being too harsh. Beth had a certain innocence. She didn't know much about the power—" she hesitated a second, then went on— "the power of carnal life. She was our mother's girl—I was left out. I think Mother was afraid of me, a little, and I remember how she hated the redness of my hair."

Aunt Lulu put her hands to her head, grabbed handfuls of her hair and pulled it straight up so she looked as if she were flying through the air. She laughed. "I found compensations.

Even though she died when Bethie was eleven and I was thirteen, Bethie continued to act as if Mother was there, her arms around her, indulging her. Helen, would you make coffee for us? I'm perishing from dryness."

As I stood in the kitchen measuring water, I jumped at a crash and turned away from the tiny faucet that always dripped. My aunt was staring at me with a wild look on her face. Beside her, a chair lay on its side; she must have leaped up violently.

"Claude!" she cried. "Why do you think he's being so damned cultivated and refined if it isn't to cover his ass! Oh, Morgan was like that, glowing with sensibility . . . oh, I know it all, the tricks to make people look elsewhere, not at the wounds. I know it all! Haven't I done it a thousand times myself? Helen. Stay clear of Claude. He's stolen a chick from a gangster's nest!"

She covered her face with her long reddish fingers. She was sobbing. "It's not that Claude isn't kind, and so smart . . . so smart. It's me," she said in a cracked voice through her hands. "Oh God! Sleep doesn't make me well! I wish I were dead!"

I pushed her to the bed, holding her arms, walking her backwards. She fell upon it, drawing up her legs beneath her. "I had a child," she mumbled.

The skin at the back of my neck prickled. I wanted to stop her mouth with my hand. But she said nothing more. I sat by the bed until I knew from her breathing that she had crept her way into some kind of sleep.

Not for the first time, I told myself I ought to move into the ballroom and try to take care of her. But the thought of it was unbearable, dreadful! That I should have left my mother's house to end up in this depressing room of decayed grandeur, a ruined room from the past, to be nurse to my mother's sister!

As I walked along Royal toward home—breathing shallowly, I had not gotten used to the humidity and at times wondered if it would drive me away from this city—I was seeing once again the young man Claude had embraced near the shadows of Pirates Alley. Was he the chick from the gangster's nest?

I thought about that as one stares into a dark corner; my thoughts were like the weakest, most flickering of candles.

My father had taken me to some caverns near Albany when I was little. I remember the slow descent, as though the earth were breathing us down into itself, the astonishment of those rooms of rock, a lake so black, so unmoving that it was like black stone.

What was I trying *not* to think about? Uncle Morgan and Claude and love. Lulu's imagined child. Gerald, weeping into the ground. And Len, whom I wanted at that moment to see with all the desperation I would have felt if that elevator which had taken my father and me into the underground cavern had vanished upwards, stranding us there forever.

One Monday morning as I was passing my aunt's place, I saw a girl peering into the entranceway. She was wearing a broom skirt. We had just gotten a shipment of them at the store. After you washed one, you were supposed to wrap it around a broom—then you didn't have to iron it. Her hair was thick and fair and fell in a faintly glamorous curve over her brow. She was slender, narrow-hipped, and her long legs were bare. She was wearing sandals like mine. She turned to smile at me. "There's a river in this place," she said.

"It's the plumbing in the bar around the corner. Nobody does anything about it."

"I'm looking for a room," she said. "Would you know of one?"

"My aunt lives here. I don't know if there are any empty rooms, but she might."

"I'm in the most terrible hole," she said. "It's just a leftover kitchen with a cot in it, really. The roaches are as big as mice. I have to get out of there. And the heat . . ."

Her accent was not southern. "You're not from around here," I noted.

"No," she replied. "I'm from near New York City. I've been here a month, exactly, today. I thought it was yesterday. I would have preferred that because Rudolph Hess crash-landed in Scotland yesterday and it would have helped me keep track. It's the only thing I manage to keep track of, months. Do you think he's insane?"

"Who?"

"Hess. I like what Churchill said: 'a case in which the imagination is baffled by the facts.' Really. That seems to me to be the case about everything."

"I don't often read the paper," I said.

Two men, talking animatedly together as they walked past us, fell silent and stared at her. She moved further into Aunt Lulu's building.

"Mercy! It really is a river," she said.

The stream from Murphy's bar was heavier than I had yet seen it. I imagined the slow weakening of the foundations of the building, the collapse, the settling and the dust.

"I have a job," she said. "Out at the air force center where they test fighter planes on Lake Pontchartrain. It's merely filing and a little typing. But I can pay a higher rent than I'm paying now."

I had a few minutes to spare before I would be late to work. The floor manager was strict about employees' being on time in the morning and not leaving a second before afternoon closing. But the hours in between passed with a certain cheerful torpor, neighborly visits among clerks, except during the busy time at midday. The manager himself liked to stop and chat with me, leaning across the counter so I was engulfed in the smell of his bayberry after-shave lotion, teasing me with vague youthful inanities about New York City where, he pretended, I had grown up and learned grand city ways. His name was Tom Elder, and I knew he wanted to ask me to meet him after work. If he did, I wondered what I'd say. He was married and he had a child. I had heard him humming "My Blue Heaven" as he strolled along the aisles, and when he passed me at my counter, he would say, distinctly: *Just Molly and me and baby makes three.*

The girl was watching me with an odd tranquillity. I said, "Come with me. We'll ask my aunt about other rooms in the building." If Lulu was asleep or recovering from a bout of drinking, that would be the end of it.

The girl followed me up the plank, the stairs, and into the ballroom.

The room seemed vast, operatic, resplendent in the radiant

morning light that masked its dinginess. Aunt Lulu was not only sober but dressed in a handsome if somewhat wrinkled suit, her hair caught in a psyche knot at the nape of her neck. She was drinking coffee, standing by a window.

"Surprised you, didn't I!" she declared heartily to me. She had. "Bank day," she said, lifting her cup in a toast. "Money day. Thank you, Father! I shall have lunch in a very good restaurant. I shall buy a pair of shoes. And Sam is coming this evening to visit. Besides all that, I will visit the mayor's office. What I've needed all along is official help in starting my repertory group." She laughed hectically. "Helen! Your aunt has been a fool! Of course I neglected the most important thing in getting started. Influence! My head has been in the clouds. I was thinking—Ibsen, Molière, Somerset Maugham, for God's sake! Who is that girl?"

Was she sober? The girl stood near the doors, her face and her body quiet, at ease.

She noticed us looking at her and started. "Oh!" she exclaimed. "I'm Nina Weir. I'm looking for a place, a room."

Lulu strode across the room, pausing only to set down her cup on the small bureau. She was taller than Nina Weir. As she stood in front of her, she seemed to stare deeply into her blonde head. The girl smiled up at her. "I must get out of the place where I'm living," she said. "It's a forgotten hole—the stove is next to the cot, and the cot is next to the door. I have a job, so I'm not a nomad. Maybe you know of a place? I was thinking I might be better off living in my car."

"You have a car?"

"A beat-up car that belonged to my grandfather. It's how I came south," she answered.

"You can live here, with me," Aunt Lulu said. "You'll have to use the cot. You might help me a little with things, so I wouldn't charge you but five dollars a week. I'll want privacy every so often. We'll manage that. I suppose you have friends you can visit. There's a sink behind that door, and a toilet behind the other one, a bathroom with a tub down the hall. It's all so simple!" She was laughing again, holding out her hands as though to say: Here! Look! Nothing to it!

Nina Weir glanced around the room, at the narrow cot, the few chairs, the bed with its hillocks of ugly chenille.

With a certain cunning, Aunt Lulu said, "Look up! Look at the ceiling. You see how the constellations have been painted across the heavens? Wonderful, isn't it? The furnishings are pretty vile, I'll grant you. But light and air are the thing, and that ceiling. This *is* New Orleans."

Nina was looking through the windows at the balcony. But I had seen her! It was she who had looked up from Royal Street on the evening when Len had walked with me to St. Phillip Street for the first time.

I realized how desperately my aunt wanted Nina to accept her offer, how much she wanted someone to be around, to be in that place with her. I had not wanted to know the depth of her desperation. I thought I knew all the phases of her drunkenness by now, but I realized, as she tried to persuade the girl to move in, that I had not known she was never truly sober. She lived in a perpetual dusk of alcohol. She was afraid, afraid that one day she would topple over and die alone, her face in the dust on the floor.

I saw Nina look at the closet with its sink like a soup bowl, at the sooty balls of dust beneath the bed, at the stained pillow ticking. She was going to refuse my aunt's offer. Len and I would continue in service.

"Yes," Nina said. "Thank you. All right."

"When?" Lulu questioned in a hard urgent voice. But it was not as hard as my heart at that moment. I saw Nina as my release, freedom.

"I've packed. I would have gone to a hotel tonight if I hadn't found a place," she said. Lulu was waving her hands about impatiently as Nina spoke.

"I mean, can you move in right away? Now? I must be first at the bank. I can't *bear* standing around. I don't lock the door. My God! How could I? There's no key. But I want to be here and show you where you must put your things."

"Yes, yes," Nina agreed hastily. "I have just two suitcases. I'll go and get them and be back in half an hour."

"Good! Splendid!" Lulu cried. "You'll have to cook for yourself. We'll keep food separate somehow. And you'll see to it that your cot is kept neat. Though I might ask you to fix me a cup of coffee or tea occasionally—you won't mind that?"

I almost warned her then, almost took her by the arm to lead her away. But I didn't.

"No—I wouldn't mind," Nina said with a graceful smile.

Nina had been deluded that first day. Even I, who knew better, hadn't sensed how fleeting, how scant, was the energy that had given my aunt an air of self-possession. It had been just enough to get her to the bank to collect her check from my grandfather's trust. She must have known, with the utterly indifferent knowledge of a drunk, that all her talk of seeking political influence in the mayor's office was a fable.

The first thing she did that day, after she had the money, was to buy liquor and pay a colored man to help her lug it to the ballroom. She hid what was left of the money in pockets of clothing, in old handbags, beneath the mattress of her bed. I imagined her singing to herself as she went about her housekeeping, nearly breathless with desire for the oblivion that lay ahead.

She almost always enjoyed that authority accorded to unreason. But in the best of circumstances, it would have been awkward for two people living in that round room, which seemed to press one toward its center as though the walls exerted a silent centripetal force. For Nina, with her gentle manners that held a faint note of atonement, Lulu's drunken howling, her black despair when she was sobering up, must have been a torment.

Nina kept hoping it would get better, she told me. And she had little experience of living around women. She had been raised by her maternal grandfather, had no living female relatives as far as she knew, and had had male tutors because her grandfather disapproved of the public schools in Tarrytown, where he and Nina lived in the gatehouse he owned on an old estate. Her mother and father had been divorced when she was two, and her mother had gone to France, where she died a few years later in Paris. Her father had disappeared. Her grandfather was a master printer. When he retired, he gave himself over to his passion for books. His taste was idiosyncratic. When she was ten years old, Nina had listened to him read from James Huneker, Boswell's *Life of Johnson*, translations from Heine, Pushkin and Joris Karl Huysmans.

He was a socialist, a follower of Eugene Debs; he'd been a pacifist during the World War. During her early adolescence, at her grandfather's fond insistence, Nina had read Elihu Burritt, William Lloyd Garrison and, of course, Gandhi. Perhaps all of this accounted for her quality of innocence, of belonging to another time and place. She was like someone who had spent years in a breakaway utopian community. Her peculiar, nar-row learning, her gleaming fairness, were mysterious and, I thought, immensely alluring.

Her grandfather died when she was eighteen. A socialist friend of his, a lawyer of fifty or so, wanted to marry Nina. She refused him, but he helped her sell the gatehouse.

Her grandfather had disapproved violently of Nina's mother. He'd wept when he received the cable from the American hos-pital in Paris where Eleanor Weir had died, but he told Nina her mother had hated the life of the mind, had given herself over to pleasure. For a long time, Nina told me, when she tried to imagine her mother, she saw her dressed like some favorite at the court of the Sun King. Her grandfather had warned her not to search for her father. There are people, he told her, who hurl themselves at life, destroying everything in their way; they are natural disasters.

It took Nina a little more than a year to find him. He had joined a religious order, taking a vow of silence. His retreat, a

Victorian pile on the banks of the Hudson River, was only a few miles from the gatehouse.

He refused to see her. She waited though, sitting on a bench in a dark hall smelling of soured wax for five hours, listening to the soft whispery steps of the brothers on the other side of the wall. Through a window, she could see a beautifully tended garden.

Her money was running out. She went to New York City, found a small apartment on Bank Street and got a job waiting on tables in a Childs restaurant. She had a brief affair with an actor, then, at a dead end, desperately missing the gatehouse and her grandfather sitting in his Morris chair in the evening, reading to her in his deep rumbling voice from a book he held in his large hands, she came to New Orleans. That particular book figured strongly in her memory. It was *Creole Sketches*, by Lafcadio Hearn.

I never met anyone so utterly independent—in the sense that she expected no one to take care of her, to do anything for her.

I was profoundly relieved when she got away from Lulu, fleeing the ballroom a month after she'd moved in, though I had my reasons for wanting her to stay there. As the days passed, I witnessed her misery. It wasn't only because of my aunt.

Sam Bridge, on one of his visits to Lulu, had met Nina and become infatuated with her. He went to the ballroom on his every leave from Fort Benning. Nina grew frantic as Lulu began to suspect Sam was not coming to see her. She took to staring at Nina like a berserk cat: silent, moon-eyed, menacing.

"You are fucking my husband, the father of my dead child,"

she shouted at Nina one evening after Sam had come and gone. Nina ran out of the ballroom and came to Gerald's. Catherine went to Claude's and told him what had happened. Nina went back to the ballroom and packed her suitcases while Lulu, too weak to stand, raged at her from the bed. When Nina was ready, she rapped with her knuckles on the doors leading to the corridor. Claude, who had been waiting just outside, entered, picked up the suitcases, and without even a glance at the bed and its raving occupant, went out of the room, Nina following.

He moved her into one of his guest rooms, where she slept in a bed upon whose headboard was painted a rose and gold and pink angel held aloft by pink clouds. The headboard was two hundred years old and had come from Paris with its owner, an ancestor of Claude's, on a ship that was captured and sunk by pirates on its return voyage to France.

I don't believe Claude wanted anyone to live with him in his house hidden behind a high wall. But when Catherine had told him of Nina's plight, he went to her at once and offered her a room for as long as she needed it.

They had met one evening at Gerald's. Marlene Lindner had been holding forth for an unbroken ten minutes that seemed a day and a night—human vanity is apparently endowed with the power to stretch time—about herself and Norman. She was a flighty person, all impulse and imagination, she confessed, while Norman was the soul of reason and honest horse-sense. Upon this theme, her voice rising excitedly, she had elaborated, speaking of the balance their marriage had achieved by the opposition of their natures, of the way Norman always brought her to her senses with his down-to-earth realism, and on she went. Norman, sitting stiffly at the table, his small cold face expressionless, more and more resembled the good-sense-benumbed nag his wife was describing. Nina stood in a shadowed corner near the fireplace, her eyes closed. I went with Gerald to get more coffee from the kitchen as Marlene paused to breathe deeply.

He started to laugh as soon as we were in the garden. "Is she driving you crazy? It's just that she's upset. That magazine that's done the story on the Quarter artists didn't take more than one picture of her. She's making up a story about Norman to make herself feel better."

"That's some story," I said.

He grinned. "She would like to be an artist, too," he said lightly. "He's the painter, so she claims the temperament."

"Is he a good painter?"

"Well—I think the trouble with him is he never met a landscape, or a worker, he couldn't paint. Easily."

When we went back, Claude was there. Marlene had fallen silent at last and was staring at her plump hands and long painted nails. Norman was describing to Catherine some device that made it possible to listen in on people's telephone conversations, "another weapon in the arsenal of state control over our lives," I heard him saying.

Nina and Claude were standing close together, talking in low voices.

After they had all gone, Catherine said, as she turned out a small iron standing lamp, that Claude had never paid her that kind of attention.

"What kind?" I asked her.

She was silent for a moment as we stood there in the darkened room. At last she said, "Artless."

A few days after Nina went to live with Claude, I met Marlene Lindner on the street. "And how are the bizarre couple on St. Ann Street in the beautiful house?" she asked, cocking her head to one side, a smile on her lips.

"They're not a couple. They're friends."

"Indeed!" she cried, emitting a cascade of foolish laughter. "I would never have guessed."

Eventually, Nina told of her childhood, the gatehouse, the books, her grandfather, at one of Gerald and Catherine's evenings. Everyone who came there had stories to tell. And no one seemed to ever tire of how it came about that Gerald broke free from the assembly line and began to write his poetry. Perhaps that was because his story was about freedom, about a new life.

CHAPTER

SEVEN

It was Sunday. Gerald had driven to Lake Pontchartrain, where he would meet his son Charles on the broad cement steps that led down to the water. They would spend an hour or so together sitting on a step, watching fishermen and talking, mostly about Charles' sister, Jean, who was a nurses' aide at Charity Hospital. Sometimes Charles wouldn't talk. Gerald himself would gradually grow silent, "like a victrola running down," he told me. Then Charles would move to a different step, then a further one, until finally he was so far away, Gerald could no longer distinguish him from other people who walked or sat by the lake.

A friend of Catherine's from Arizona, a teacher, had come to the city for a visit, and Catherine was to meet her for lunch at a restaurant. She had put on lipstick and patted circles of darkish powder on her cheeks and her forehead that looked like little brown pancakes. I brushed her face with my hand so that the powder would be more evenly distributed. "It's what they wear back home," she said, giggling slightly. "She'll be wearing a hat. I haven't got one. But if I don't put on powder, she'll think I've gone to the dogs."

I stood at the doorway of the little room where Gerald worked, intending only to look. Then I went in. On a single shelf below the window that looked out on the wild garden, there were volumes of poetry: Chaucer, the *Odyssey* and the *Iliad*, Keats, Walt Whitman, William Carlos Williams, Hart Crane, John Donne, and several anthologies whose covers bore small photographs of poets, each one inside a medallion. A Remington portable typewriter and some copybooks of the sort I had used in school were on the table. A pencil lay across a long sheet of paper. The paper was covered with lists of words.

I had imagined poets caught their poems from the air. How could rhyme and sense come together so wholly, so like a thing in nature? So that it seemed the poem could only have already been there, a thing to be found?

But the lists of words—there were many yellow sheets in a pile covered with more lists in Gerald's tiny distinct printing— suggested humble labors I had not conceived of.

Partly out of a superstitious belief that my presence would have left a trace, partly from curiosity, I told Gerald I had gone into his room. He didn't appear to mind at all. I asked him about the word lists. "It's practicing," he answered. "Poems are found and then made."

During the months I lived in New Orleans, I loved more people than I had ever loved in my life. I drowned in waters of love. My heart beat strongly in anticipation of seeing them. I never wearied of their faces, their voices.

There were a few I didn't like: the Lindners, a young pianist, David Hamilton, who was a friend of Claude's, and Tom Elder, the floor manager at the store. But if I had loved them all, I would have been carried off to an insane asylum, deranged by exaltation. Nina was among those I cared for most, though I had so heartlessly tried to slip her into my place as my aunt's keeper.

I told her about Len soon after she moved into the ballroom, and heard myself altering circumstances as I went along. I didn't want to convey to Nina—to admit openly—my confusion about his tie to my aunt. I wanted her to like him. I was visiting Lulu the evening Nina and Len met. As far as I could tell, Lulu had not had much to drink, but her mood was cranky and imperious, though she was still bent on charming Nina so that when she spoke to her, her voice softened slightly and grew as winsome as she could make it.

Len had brought some shrimp wrapped in paper that he had taken from the restaurant where he was working at the moment. As soon as he entered the room, my aunt began to reproach him loudly.

"For God's sake, you spoiled boy! Ever since you cooked up that mess in my little frying pan, I've not been able to use it. I expect you to clean it! Really, I wish you wouldn't treat my home like a hobo camp."

"That was a mess I cooked for you," Len said neutrally.

"What has that to do with what I'm referring to?"

He held out the shrimp to her. She gazed at it loftily, then selected one and brushed away the grains of rice that clung to it.

"I suppose you pinched this from a customer's leftovers."

"No, I didn't. I took it from the kitchen."

"Len," I called.

He turned to me. I was sitting on the cot next to Nina, who was sewing a button on a white blouse of hers.

"Hello, Helen." He glanced at Nina.

I introduced them. They smiled politely at each other. For the brief time he stayed, they didn't speak. I saw him look at her from time to time as he wrangled with Lulu.

"What do you think?" I asked Nina when we had a moment alone. My aunt had gone off to take a bath, complaining bitterly that she would, she knew, find the tub filthy because the other tenants in the building were all dirty rubes.

"He seems pleasant," she said. She must have seen my disappointment for she added quickly, "And that hair is wonderful—like the breast feathers of some bird. I like the way he looks, so private, like he'd have thoughts you'd want to know about but he might not tell you."

But in the weeks that followed, she appeared to develop a dislike for him. If he came to the ballroom or to Gerald's and sat near her, she would move away as far as she could get from him. When Gerald drove us to the delta at the end of June, she squeezed herself tightly into the corner of the backseat of his old Ford. I could see how stiff, how uncomfortable she was. I knew it was because Len was sitting between us. It was so unlike her to rebuff anyone, even Marlene Lindner, who treated her with such gross condescension.

I admired her unjudgmental stillness, a little like Gerald's, among other people, and the way she listened to them, as Ger-

ald did, deferentially. She made me aware of the restlessness of
my own mind, which hardly ever seemed empty of comment
and argument, of convictions that rattled around in my brain,
which I suspected were ruled by feelings that bore little connection with them.

"Why don't you like him?" I asked her once.

"It's not that, not dislike," she replied. "Your aunt is so unhappy, and she speaks to him in such a cruel way. It makes me
feel strange."

"Strange, how?"

She looked at me helplessly. "I don't know," she answered.

I pressed her, but it did no good. I was in love with Len. I
didn't know how he felt about me, or rather, I thought I knew
one moment, but not the next. Nina's response to him alarmed
me. It was like a bad omen.

Nina was having an affair with Sam Bridge. She told me about it
a few days after she had moved into Claude's house.

On Saturdays when we both worked only half the day, we
took po'boy sandwiches to the banks of the Mississippi near the
French Market and spent peaceable hours there together. Our
meandering accounts to each other of the week just past would
begin as we unwrapped the wax paper from our lunches.
Events that had seemed trivial and random at the time would
be seen to have continuity and meaning, if it was only in the
telling of them. I had not had so close and affectionate a friend-
ship with a woman before.

I reported that Tom Elder had left me a note inside a petti-
coat on the counter of the underwear section. It consisted

solely of the lyric of a popular song with "Sometimes I wonder why I spend the lonely hours . . ." heavily underlined in red pencil. I laughed. Her head was turned away from me. "Nina?"

"I've gotten into an awful situation. With Sam Bridge."

I was stirred and frightened, and for a mad second I imagined my aunt had crept up behind us to listen.

"But—in the ballroom?" I thought of the two of them—his uniform laid out neatly across a chair, her cornflower blue dress that I had gotten for her at a discount, flung on the cot—listening in thrilled terror for Lulu's heavy tread coming up the stairs, though it was hard to imagine urbane Sam as either thrilled or terrified.

"We went to Mississippi," she said. "He came to visit Lulu. I was in bed. She was asleep. She'd eaten so much crab Louis that Len brought her and drunk so much beer, she was completely out."

She and Sam had whispered about Lulu. His questions were increasingly senseless, "only to keep me talking," Nina said. He had sat at the foot of her cot. She had drawn up the sheet to cover herself, up to her neck. "Let's drive to Pass Christian in your car," he'd suddenly said.

"There was that awful magic—when it's the middle of the night and you feel you can go anywhere. That's really why I went with him. He didn't know it was that, not that it would have mattered. He wanted to get me out of the ballroom, alone with him."

Sam had noted her worried stare at Lulu snoring in her bed. It wouldn't make a bit of difference to her, he told Nina.

"I asked, 'What won't?' He said, 'Anything at all.'" She told him that Lulu was angry with her most of the time as it was, and obviously regretted inviting her to live in the ballroom. Sam said Lulu invented her life, except for the drinking part of it, that she made up stories—like the imaginary infant—and that no one was real to her, nothing was real save the immense momentary lift of her first drink of the day.

"Then I touched his hand. I said, 'You're real.' When I did that, I knew I was going with him. I should not have touched him."

They drove through dark hours into a pale rose dawn. The trip felt watery, as though they were in a boat, not a car. The road passed along bays, over streams where floating patches of lavender hyacinths caught and held the first light of the sun in their petals. Behind narrow strands of beach, Nina saw the tropical rich moist green of trees that appeared to move forward toward the water, their naked roots hard and brown in soft banks of damp dark soil. She pretended she was on a motoring trip with her grandfather. Sam told her stories of his residency years. "Of course, they had that grisly fascination medical stuff has—the inside of the body, that has no self."

When he mentioned Lulu, not often, it was with the utter indifference of a man who has lost every trace of interest in a woman he once thought he cared about. "Then I was horrified to be in the car, on my way to a bed in a hotel."

The hotel he took her to was like a plantation house. Across from it was the Gulf, sparkling like mica, and an empty beach. He took a vast room on the first floor. "You can't imagine how he sounded," she said. "As though he owned the world. The desk clerk didn't even look at me."

There were tall windows in the room, covered with shuttered blinds that let in narrow streams of light. She had no bathing suit. They had passed some small shops in the lobby, one of which displayed beachwear. "We'll have breakfast," he told her, "and then I'll get you a suit."

In the dining room they were brought grapefruit halves resting on beds of ice. The colored waiter's bowtie was askew under his chin. His shoes squeaked and she looked down at them. She'd been noticing the feet of colored people ever since she'd come south. "They've been pressed down to the earth so hard," she said. "And the weight of what they carry tortures their feet."

Despite the fact that it was Sunday and the lobby stores were closed, Sam got the telephone number of the woman who owned the beachwear shop from the desk clerk, called her and persuaded her to come to the hotel and open it just long enough for him to choose and buy a jade-green two-piece suit for Nina.

"Except for Claude—and he wouldn't have tried—nobody I've ever known could have gotten away with that," she said. "The presumption. My grandfather would have called it bourgeois tyranny of the trivial sort. Fiddle-faddle . . ."

They went to the beach, where there were a few people now lying on the sand. Sam suggested a stroll before swimming. She knew he was showing her off, "like booty," she said.

In the water, Sam wore a thin white rubber cap. It billowed as he swam. She was oppressed by everything, his parading her in front of the sunbathers, bullying the woman into opening her shop, the membranous white bladder of his bathing cap, the suddenly gone-dead voice in which he had addressed the old waiter, and she detested herself for conspiring with him for the brief excitement of giving in to an impulse.

They returned to the shuttered room. He pulled the cover from the bed and turned down the heavy linen sheet. She had found the water too warm. The whole earth was too warm. She stood in the middle of the room, the salt drying on her skin, not knowing what to do. There was a smell of jasmine in the warm stillness.

"It was strange. For a moment the room seemed empty. We were both absent—just for that moment. Then he came to me and slipped a strap of the suit from my shoulder. His hand was chilled from the water. Somehow we managed the huge distance to the bed. Miles. The buckle of his trunks scraped my hip. I noticed a rose embroidered on the pillowcase. Things stood out in that unreal way they do before you faint. I was stunned when he put his hand between my legs and grabbed my bottom and lifted me up as though he were going to roll me into a ball."

She stared at me. "There's something frightful about sex," she said. "Yet you want it. The frightfulness gets swallowed up so quick. It is like some monstrous shadow pausing for a split second at the window—then you pull down the shade."

"Weren't you told sex was beautiful?" I asked. My throat was dry. I had meant to sound ironic, but I only sounded timid.

"I wasn't told anything," she said. "But I had a friend when I was quite little, and we drew male and female sexual organs on the backs of some paper dolls. As it turned out, the drawings were quite accurate." She smiled. A certain intentness and strain had gone away from her face. I think she had passed the strain on to me. My hands shook slightly as I folded the wax paper from the sandwich into smaller and smaller squares. I was thinking about my aunt.

In the hotel, to Sam's amusement, Nina had remade the bed. As they left the room, she turned to look back at it. She had not noticed until then a rug with a pattern of anemones and thick green vines, or the dressing table with three mirrors.

"It was so luxurious. I loved it. I hadn't known that about myself—that I would love such a place." Sam mistook her silent appraisal of the room as sentiment concerning himself. He began to caress her back and thighs in full view of an elderly couple who had just emerged from a room down the hall. Nina sprang out of his reach. He laughed. The old couple stood there, visibly shocked.

"My grandfather was right about middle-class people," Nina said. "They adore themselves and they're indifferent to how they're seen. That's why they can behave brutally and crudely. Sam is so civil, you wouldn't guess he could act that way."

"*They?* I expect my father was middle-class. He wasn't like that. And all my mother thinks about is how she is seen."

"I meant, mostly," she said stubbornly. "Claude isn't like that either. In a way, he isn't middle-class."

"I daresay Claude has his crude moments."

"I know that. But no matter what he does, his thoughts about himself aren't—" she paused, searching for a word— "triumphant." I didn't know what she meant. I didn't care to reflect on Claude's crude moments.

"Didn't you feel something for Sam?"

"Reluctantly. How can I speak of it? Does the word *sex* convey that moment when you've slipped over a line and are carried away?"

"Yes."

She laughed and pushed my hair behind my ears and looked at me. "You dear," she said.

Sam hadn't stopped talking on the drive back to New Orleans. He'd been boisterous, immensely cheerful. As they drew closer to the city, Nina became terribly frightened. She asked him to park her car on the corner of Gerald's street, and to leave her at once.

"Don't be afraid of Lulu," he told her. "She'll sense it. Fear arouses her. She'll go wild."

"How can I not be what I am?" she had asked him.

He'd clasped her neck with his hand. "Do as I say," he'd commanded her, smiling.

They had spoken of Claude, whom Sam had known from the time they were boys. Claude was two years older. When Sam was a resident at a New Orleans hospital, he'd treated Claude for gonorrhea.

"He leads a perilous life," Sam had told Nina. "Now he's mixed up with an Italian kid."

"Lulu said something about that," I interjected.

"Claude's so composed. He's like a royal person in a royal coach traveling across his own domain. But the whole back of the coach is missing so you can look in and see everything. Everyone who knows him seems to know about the boy."

I told her about seeing Claude and the dark-haired young man that evening near Pirates Alley.

"Sam said the boy's father is a smuggler and a criminal, probably in the Black Hand, which is a kind of criminal kingdom inside the country. They've always had power in Louisiana. Fifty years ago, they had the chief of police killed. Sam said they aren't the other side of the coin—they *are* the coin.

"The boy's father had him tracked to Claude's house. The man that followed him found him naked beneath the piano—Sam said incubating more gonococcus, no doubt—asleep in Claude's arms. He would have had Claude killed then and there, but there's some reform group investigating the Black Hand, and so the old man had to deprive himself of murder for the time being. Sam says there have been other reform groups and investigations, but they never come to anything. There's another son, who killed a labor union fellow in Baton Rouge. He's living in Cuba.

"Claude was awake. He saw the man staring at him through the French doors. He looked just like a big toad, he told Sam."

She paused and glanced at me. I could feel my lips curled and tight against my teeth. Was she waiting for me to shout or scream or wave my arms about in protest?

"It's all so awful, Nina. Can't anyone stop anything? Do we float along helplessly? Why can't Claude go away?"

She didn't reply, only shook her head slowly. My boring easy days in the store, the evenings with Gerald and Catherine, my yearning for Len, my blue-and-yellow room, my entire daily life had been dimming, shrinking with frightening rapidity as she had been telling me about herself and Sam, about Claude and the boy and those murderous men. I no longer imagined my aunt creeping up on us but men like toads, armed with guns. The stories I had heard in the house on St. Phillip Street had filled me up, like one of Gerald's suppers, with contentment, with a sense of the variousness of people, with a sense of being in a safe place. But there were stories that can make you tremble with apprehension, with the knowledge of the frailty of your own life—that cut you out of life.

I longed to obliterate these new stories I had heard and to be with Nina in my plain small room where the wood floor kept warm from the heat of the day long into the evening.

Gerald could make Nina laugh. She would lose some of that seriousness of hers that I thought of as especially youthful somehow, and she would become playful, as Gerald was, with his sweet, teasing voice and homely jokes that didn't push you away but took you in.

"Sam was almost blithe," she said. "He's fond of Claude— it's probably a class thing, and they were boys together—but he doesn't seem to give a damn what might happen to him. Or else he believes Claude deserves a terrible fate. You can't tell what people really think about *that*."

"Sometimes you can," I said, recalling the words of the desk clerk at the hotel where I'd stayed, and the stableboy I had overheard so many years before.

"Sam said a cold and awful thing. He said, 'Claude goes where his cock leads him. It is an organ without a brain cell, all blind urgent desire.' And he reached over and took my hand and said, 'As you know.' Oh! I hated him at that moment!"

"But, Nina!" I cried out. "You're living there with Claude! You're in danger!"

She began to eat her sandwich. Her skin glowed in the sunlight, her wheaten hair fell across her forehead as she bent to bite into the long loaf. After a moment, she said calmly, "I do think of that. The first night I moved in, while I was putting my things away, Claude came into the room and sat down and told me about those men. I didn't mention what I'd already heard, or that Sam had said I was crazy to move there. Claude was so cool. He might have been telling me the history of some old house down the street. He said I was safe. The boy's father is only interested in him. And then he said, 'Perhaps it will all die away long before I do.' I was so confused, and embarrassed, too, at what he'd told me, I felt obliged to even things out somehow, so I told him about Sam and me, and going to Pass Christian, and the rest of it. And he said, 'When we give our favors, we must bear the consequences.' Then he made me an omelet. I told him I'd already eaten. He said, 'Never mind, the complications of love will make you lose weight.'"

She finished her sandwich. "I did eat it," she went on. "The kitchen is beautiful, like the rest of the house. You'll have to come and see it. There's a pale gray Japanese bowl on the kitchen table and he keeps fruit in it. Even if he's just eating crackers, he puts them on porcelain plates he inherited from his mother. He's like that, ceremonial."

He's vain, I thought to myself.

"Every night that he's home, he drinks something before he goes to bed. He doesn't sleep well. He stands up to drink it, very formal, in the kitchen. I've seen him with a tall glass filled with something the color of smoke. David Hamilton says the glass is leaded crystal, but he doesn't know what Claude drinks either. I told David I thought it might be milk and sherry, and

David lifted his eyebrow and curled his lip—I'm sure he's seen some movie actor do that—and said, 'Claude, drink milk? Are you mad!' Anyhow, I asked Claude. And he said it was a libation to the god of nightmares."

"No wonder—after what you've told me!"

"No, no. Not to stop him from having nightmares. He was *asking* for them, but that they come to him only in his dreams."

"And does he have nightmares?" I asked.

"Nearly every night. He hopes there won't be any in his waking life, and he includes me now in that hope."

She smiled and looked happy, so incredibly happy, as though she'd been given a great gift, a thing her heart desired.

When the smile had faded, she said, "He doesn't always go right to bed after his libation. Sometimes he goes out. Then, he doesn't come back until the sky is the same color as what he drinks."

"What did he mean about *it* dying before he does?"

"His passion for the boy," she replied.

"So he won't go away or stop seeing him?"

"No."

CHAPTER

EIGHT

Two waist-high drinking fountains stood in the store on either side of the elevator to the second floor. Above each one was a printed sign. One read White, the other Colored.

It was Saturday, a few minutes before the noon closing, and I was watching the entrance to the store for Nina. She was to come and pick me up. Before we had lunch, we were going to Basin Street, to a graveyard where Marie Laveau, the New Orleans Voodoo Queen, was buried in a crypt. Claude had told Nina she might see a believer in black magic, of whom there were many, he said, come and mark the Queen's crypt with an *X* for good luck. Then we were going to look at some old houses Catherine had told me about. The historian she typed for three mornings a week had just completed a chapter on the architecture of New Orleans, and she had made a list of Greek Revival houses she thought Nina and I would like to see. Nina said that for the rest of the afternoon she would like to eat plates of cray-fish and drink bourbon. I took it that Sam Bridge wouldn't be in town for the weekend.

Exactly at noon, Nina came through the door wearing her blue dress. I saw her glance over at the fountains and at once walk quickly to them. She bent over the one marked Colored, turned the metal knob and opened her mouth to receive the spray of water. There was an immediate flurry of movement at the counters nearest her as salesclerks left their posts and went hesitantly toward Nina, all except Tom Elder, who ran down the aisle with mincing steps, his bottom shaking. I hastily left my counter to go to her.

"She drank at the colored!" cried Miss Beauregard as I passed her standing behind her perfume counter. Tom Elder and the clerks who had converged on Nina were glaring at her. She stared back, her face pale, drops of water around her mouth. She did not look defiant but patient and determined.

"You can't do that," Tom Elder said. "You-all *know* you can't do that!"

"Nasty manners," muttered a saleswoman I didn't know.

"Unless you-all can't read," Tom was saying. "If that's it, let me inform you that you are severely insulting our colored cus-tomers. That is *their* fountain!"

"I can read," Nina said in a loud trembling voice. "And I hate what I read."

"Nobody cares what you hate!" Tom Elder shouted sud-denly. The salesclerks stepped back, away from Nina. I ran to her, gripped her arm with both my hands and pulled her to the entrance and out onto the sidewalk.

"What are you doing?" I cried.

"I don't know," she said wildly, moving her head back and forth as though I were clutching her neck rather than her arms. I let go.

"It makes me desperate when I see those signs."

"You've seen the ones in the store before."

"Yes. But I've been thinking about them."

"You can't change anything that way."

"How *do* you change anything then?"

People eddied around us. "Oh, come on, let's walk," I said. I hadn't put my stock away. I hadn't clocked myself out. What would people say to me on Monday? I had read anger and fear in the faces of the clerks as they looked at Nina. It was all very well for Gerald to spend an hour with his colored neighbor, the two of them sitting fifteen feet apart in their chairs, talking to each other. But Gerald was a poet. Poets could do things other people couldn't.

"And you can't change things by wearing nickels in your ears either," I said. I started to laugh and was relieved to see her smile. Catherine had met her walking down St. Ann Street last week with a nickel in her ear. She had explained she had seen colored children carrying their streetcar fare that way.

"It seemed so convenient," she had said. "You don't have to carry a pocketbook."

I thought of Len. When he was eight or nine, he'd joined a group of colored children who were dancing for money on a Chicago street corner. He had taken off his shoes and socks in preparation for the dance, as they had, and stuck bottle caps on his toes. People threw pennies at them and they all shared in the take. Len was overjoyed. Every day for nearly a week, after school, he would race from his home to find the dancing troupe. On Friday afternoon, his father, the rabbi, looking for Len so as to bring him home before sunset, discovered his pale little child among the dark-skinned dancers. "He nearly fainted," Len told me. All the way home, the rabbi, keeping a firm hold of Len's hand as though he might run away, kept telling Len he was a Jew, that he should be charitable to Negroes, to anyone less fortunate than himself—but no dancing in the street, never any dancing.

"I don't want to see the Voodoo Queen's grave," Nina declared. "Let's go right away to that café on Bourbon Street."

"But maybe we could look at the houses Catherine mentioned." I wanted the day to be as we had planned it, though I knew it couldn't be now. The air was leaden, the sky had clouded over. I recalled Miss Beauregard's face, usually placid, even kindly. It was as if she'd sprung at me from behind her counter wearing a fiend's mask at the moment Nina had raised her face from the drinking fountain.

"They'll die in this war that's coming, just like everyone else," Nina said after we'd ordered our lunch. "My insides tremble when I see those signs. Gerald says, 'patience, patience.' He means laws. But the mutilation now!"

She took a small bite of the fish she'd ordered.

"Who caught this fish!" she exclaimed.

"Anyone could have," I replied hastily. "Do you think only colored people catch fish?"

"But what do you think?" she asked, looking at me sharply. "You haven't said anything. You're worried. You've been trying to calm me down. Why don't people say what they think? Claude says they *don't*—that it's not American to think." She laughed briefly, irritably.

"I've heard him say that," I said. "Are you some kind of communist?" I asked, smiling.

"If I were, I'd get a little of that Moscow gold I've heard about and buy myself a good pocketbook and find a room of my own."

"Is it hard, living at Claude's?"

"Yes. I'm in the way. I know he'd rather have his house to himself. We're too delicate with each other. It's a strain for both of us. But then, it's wonderful, too, the talks we have, even the effort we both must make."

For a while we ate and didn't talk. She put down her fork and reached over the table to touch my hand with hers.

"Helen, what do you feel when you see a Negro going to that particular fountain to drink?"

Had I ever noticed? I couldn't recall. "I don't think I've seen anyone use the colored fountain," I replied. "But I don't keep an eye on it."

"They probably make sure they've had all the water they want before they come to the store," she said as though speaking to herself.

"Really—I don't remember ever seeing a colored person in the store." She was looking at me reflectively.

"Things aren't cheap at Fountain's," I added uneasily.

"Oh, yes, there's that," she said. She smiled at me with her customary graceful sweetness. Her head was inclined slightly forward, toward me, as though anything I might say would be interesting. It was her form of tact. My mother often spoke about her own tact, calling it the foundation of good manners. She hoped I would have good manners, too. As I grew older, as I went more often to the homes of school friends, I saw other ways of being and behaving. I'd concluded that Mother's tact consisted of keeping herself free from other people's discomfort. I wondered if I hadn't learned that lesson too well.

"It was an impulse," Nina said. "I didn't stop to think about the trouble it might make for you. I'm sorry."

"I don't think it will make trouble," I said. "They'll forget."

For a few days they didn't forget. Tom Elder asked me if my friend loved niggers.

"I don't see how you can love a whole group of people," I responded nervously and coldly. "She's from another place, and she's not used to the way it is down here."

"'Down here,'" he mimicked me. "That's how you people think of us—that we're 'down here'—like we're in some ugly hole in the ground."

I refused to talk with him about it any more. Miss Beauregard was distinctly unfriendly to me, but I caught her staring at me from behind the perfume bottles with avidity, and I thought to myself that she would like to have torn me to bits with questions.

"Your shoes are covered with mold," she observed a few mornings after Nina had gone to the colored fountain. We were in the staff room and she was applying rouge to her large cottony cheeks. "Lookit the green stuff all over your heels. You ought to wipe them off every day. Don't you know yet what our weather is like?"

I took a handkerchief from my pocketbook and rubbed at my shoes. "Look what you're doing to that nice hanky," she clucked. I looked up at her, meeting her intent stare. I realized I had become both disgusting and fascinating to her.

"You ought to come by and visit me some Sunday," she said. "So you can see a nice southern home. I've got twenty-eight sweaters I've collected I could show you. We could have tea."

I saw for the first time that she was a young woman. I had thought of her as middle-aged, partly because she was so shapeless in her print cotton dresses. Her face had a hectic pinkness from the rouge she had applied thickly. Her sandy eyebrows were raised high as she stared at me, and her pale hazel eyes were wide with some excitement. I thought—she wants me to bring Nina to her house. She wants to know something. I felt a faraway pity for her, locked in with her twenty-eight sweaters, feeling things she couldn't find a language for. And I felt pity for myself, too, for a moment, for my irresoluteness, the shapelessness of my thoughts, like Miss Beauregard's body. Only Nina was free.

"Thank you," I said. "Perhaps I will."

"That'll be just grand," she said shrilly.

But I never did get to see her nice southern home.

Nina had not returned to the ballroom since she had left to go to Claude's house. For some time after that she worried about the possibility of running into Aunt Lulu. She was reluctant to go near Royal Street.

"She forced you out," I said. "You shouldn't be afraid to look her in the face."

"But I am," Nina replied. "When the shock wore off, I was able to think about it. It was my fault, really. The moment I walked into that room, I knew moving there was a bad idea. It's true I had to get out of that place I was in, but I could have kept on looking. The thing was, it seemed easy at the time, and I was curious about you and about her. She has a real reason for hating me now."

"She's not Sam's wife anymore."

"Oh, Helen—" she began.

It was at that moment that I glanced up and saw Aunt Lulu walking slowly toward us, across Jackson Square to where Nina and I had been sitting on a bench, talking. Accompanying my aunt, his arm linked with hers, was an elderly man in a blue suit with a vest, a fringe of heavy yellowish mustache hiding his mouth like a muzzle. His skin was red and grainy and his pale blue eyes were open and staring like a doll's. Nina stood up at once as though to run away.

"Girls!" exclaimed my aunt, smiling broadly. "How sweet to see you two here!" She was wearing her money-day suit. Her hair was caught up in a snood made of thick green thread. As they came closer, I imagined they tottered slightly.

"Here's my darling niece, Helen, and a young friend of mine, Nina Blake. I want you to meet Mr. Metcalf, an acquaintance of mine—"

"My last name is Weir," Nina said somewhat breathlessly.

"Oh, my awful memory! Of course. Weir. Mr. Metcalf is visiting New Orleans for a few days." She winked broadly, but whether it was at the memorial to the Battle of New Orleans behind our bench or at us, I couldn't tell.

"Do have a drink with us," Mr. Metcalf suggested, following his words with a low grinding chuckle.

"Mr. Metcalf is a very important official with the United Fruit Company," Aunt Lulu said emphatically. "And do join us for a drink!"

"Um . . ." said Mr. Metcalf.

When Aunt Lulu said *United Fruit*, I recollected the desk clerk proclaiming that the Quarter was "full of fruits," and a surge of laughter rose in my throat. I barely managed to imprison it behind a grin I knew was rigid, like a jack-o'-lantern's. I stared fixedly at Mr. Metcalf's mustache, in which I was sure I detected the tiny amber claw of some crustacean whose other parts he must have consumed for lunch.

"We were just leaving," I heard Nina say to my aunt's smiling face. "We may even be late, so——" My aunt was waving her hand in dismissal like royalty. "Go ahead, girls," she said with magnanimity.

They turned away from us and headed in one direction until Mr. Metcalf, with a strange childish obstinacy, stood stock still while Aunt Lulu ineffectually pushed and pulled at his stooped shoulders. Suddenly he yanked her in the opposite direction.

"My God!" I gasped. "What's holding them up?"

"The pilgrimage," Nina said. "To the Holy Grail overflowing with bourbon."

"It makes me feel dreadful, seeing her like that," I said, but I was laughing convulsively. Nina shook me. "Well—she didn't try to kill me," Nina said.

"She's forgotten," I said, coughing.

"Let's go look at the Cathedral," she suggested. "Then I have to leave you. I'm meeting Sam at Charity Hospital. He's going to take me to see an operation. A friend of his is the surgeon."

"Lord! What do you want to do that for?"

"I want to see," she replied serenely.

I owed my mother a letter and I had some clothes to wash. I liked hanging them up to dry on the cord in Gerald's garden. If I pressed my face against the damp cloth, I could smell a somewhat muted aroma of gardenias, a delirious and romantic aroma even when mixed with Ivory soap.

Gerald and Catherine were out somewhere. I finished my tasks and decided to go for a walk. It was late in the afternoon, and I thought to walk right into the dusk, a time I loved best in the Quarter, when I felt carried along as though in a warm perfumed stream in the tender waning of the daylight.

As I neared Toulouse Street, Len came from around the corner, lighting a cigarette. I took in everything about him with a glance, his thin hands cupped around a match, his silver hair, a rip in the right-hand pocket of his trousers, his pale wide forehead.

It had been a week since I'd seen him one evening at the Lindners' apartment. They had invited people for coffee and political revelations, these latter delivered with their customary air of bringing civilization to the natives. The only person they didn't try to instruct in how to view the perfidiousness of capitalism was Gerald. "They know I can't be saved," he told me.

That evening they also wanted us to see a pair of shoes some friend in New York City had sent Norman after he had mailed him the most precise measurements of every part of each of his feet. The shoes would revolutionize footwear, Norman said, and put an end to the destruction of human feet by greedy shoe manufacturers, abetted by the vanity of the self-aggrandizing bourgeoisie. I had seen Len glance quickly, as I had, at the open-toed spikes Marlene was wearing on her small broad feet.

Did we know, asked Norman, that upper-class Chinese women were obliged to have their feet bound only in order to show they did no physical labor? And that British policemen wore those tall helmets to intimidate the British working class, who were, in any case, stunted by deprivation?

Norman produced the shoes. The leather was the color of bullfrogs and had been formed into rigid bumps to accommodate each toe. The shoes looked extraordinarily primitive, like extinct burrowing animals. Norman snatched off his sneakers and showed us how perfectly his new shoes fit him. "Marvelous!" he insisted.

"I don't think they'll appeal to either the bourgeoisie or the working class," Gerald had remarked lightly. "How much do they cost?"

"Now, Gerry, you're not a political animal. How would you know what appeals to different classes? You don't even think there *are* classes in the USA."

Norman didn't reveal the price and Gerald didn't press him.

"What did you think of those hideous objects Norman showed us?" I asked Len as we walked along Bourbon.

"I think Norman may abandon the revolution and devote the rest of his life to his feet," Len replied.

"It's maddening—the way people with views about everything under the sun talk in that *of course* way—as if what they profess is irresistible. My mother is a bit like that."

"I do think, though, that Norman is very fond of Gerald, even though he's so edgy about personal feeling. It's easy enough to love Chinese peasants thousands of miles away."

My heart thumped in my ears when he said *personal feeling*.

"Don't you think he has personal feeling about Marlene?"

"He sees her as another aspect of himself."

"In those high heels?"

Len laughed. He said, "Are you hungry? It's a little early but still . . . shall we have supper together at Florian's?"

I agreed at once, and in a few minutes we were sitting in the booth where Nina and I often sat. A few men were drinking at the bar, speaking in low voices. It was too early in the evening for rowdiness.

"Nina and I come here a lot," I said shyly.

"How is she?"

"She spent the afternoon with Sam watching an operation at Charity Hospital."

He looked startled. "What did she want to do that for? Well—it's like her, I suppose. She's a Martian—everything on earth is a novelty. I wonder if she holds opinions about anything."

I told him about the drinking-fountain incident.

"Yes. That's an opinion," he said. "Do the Lindners know about it?"

"Gerald told them. Marlene said Nina was an infantile bourgeois romantic."

"She would. I feel like a shot of liquor. Do you?"

I nodded. If he had said arsenic, I would have agreed. I had sat in bars with him before. Something was different. From moment to moment, my mood changed. I wanted to laugh out loud for a long time. My skin felt electric. I thought—does he know I am crazy at this moment? I began to talk about Nina; the subject was like a resting place.

She had followed a colored boy. He was holding a bunch of cherries, eating them one by one. She trailed him around the Quarter to Rampart. Now and then, a cherry would fall to the sidewalk. "Like Hansel and Gretel," commented Len.

"Well, it was the next day she came to get me at Fountain's, and caused all that excitement by drinking from the colored fountain."

"She continued to follow him," he remarked. He saw me glancing at the list of prices on the menu. "Have it all. I've worked five straight nights and I'm loaded and I'm taking you." He gave me what I could only judge to be an encouraging smile. I was very unhappy, and unhappier still when he said he'd seen Aunt Lulu in this very place for the first time. I told him about meeting Mr. Metcalf. "He's one of her drinking friends," he said. "He comes to the city on business. I met him not long after meeting Lulu. He offered me a job."

"What sort of job?" I had not meant to sound suspicious, but so I had sounded. He looked faintly puzzled.

"He was too drunk to be very clear. I think it was to go and do something magisterial in some Central American country. He kept repeating that I'd love it there. I could live like an emperor."

I was listening, but my attention was elsewhere. I was trying to prevent myself from asking him outright if he had made love to my aunt. He came from a family coiled and tight with purpose. Had Lulu seemed to him the embodiment of freedom? A woman throwing her life away? I put my hand over my mouth. He stared at me curiously.

His hand reached out and gently pulled my hand from my mouth. "What do you want to say?" he asked softly. I was afraid I would weep; I shook my head, unable to speak. I was saved from watery disintegration by the waitress, who placed in front of us the fish stew we had both ordered. I picked up a slice of white bread and pressed it to my cheek. He pretended not to notice and began to speak of his father.

"He's a baffling mix, always telling us we must be able to get along in the world, accommodate ourselves—only fools fail at that—but he kept a photograph of the Scottsboro boys tacked above his desk. Did you know that the youngest boy, Heywood Patterson, was thirteen years old? It took the jury twenty-five minutes to convict him. Poppa showed me a newspaper picture of a lynched man, a poor bundle of rags at the end of a rope, shrunken as though his flesh had been clamped right to his bones by some terrible instrument. It made me feel weak. How could there be success in the world? For anyone?"

I had heard about the Scottsboro boys. Perhaps in school. I thought of Nina following the boy with the cherries, then, as Len said, following him in her mind, and the idea of it leading her right to that colored drinking fountain.

"*South* was the abomination to my father. When I told him I was coming here, he said I might as well visit a village the morning after a pogrom."

I hesitated. I looked into Len's face and the truth flew out of me. "I don't know what a pogrom is," I said.

He hardly seemed surprised. He told me his father had fled from Kishinev, a village in Russia, after a pogrom that lasted three days in which forty-five Jews had been killed. As he spoke, another landscape eclipsed the mild Hudson Valley hills and the fragrant breathy streets of the Quarter. I imagined a village huddled to the earth, horsemen, chickens running crazily, a dense forest, people fleeing, dogs prowling among dead bodies.

"It was partly why my father's feelings were so strong about slavery, about Negroes. Also, it's something in his temperament. Suffering doesn't lead inevitably to sympathy for others. Often enough, it has the opposite effect. But he is also afraid of Negro people, their darkness, their hiddenness. We had a Negro maid, or an occasional cook. He didn't know what to say to them—or what they might suddenly say to him. So he always overpays. It's very mixed up in him. In most people who think about it at all, I suppose."

We spoke of other things. I told him that Gerald had been invited to give readings of his poetry in New York and Boston and other cities, that he wanted to go but couldn't see how to accumulate the cash what with all he had to send his wife.

We spoke of our affection for Gerald. Our conversation was running down in protestations of love for someone who was, to me, suddenly a shadow.

The men at the bar grew noisier. We joked a little about Lulu and Mr. Metcalf, and Len said, "Wait until she tells him about knowing Anna Held and Will Rogers, if she hasn't already."

"Will that truly matter to Mr. Metcalf?" I asked, smiling, and so we conspired to turn my aunt into a figure of fun.

I was hardly aware of time passing as we walked to where he lived, as though *here* was at once followed by *there*. The stairs on the third floor were unlit. The house was shabby and old and neglected. His room was bare and neat. His presence surrounded me like a second skin.

There was a moment when my hand lay upon the small of his back and I imagined Lulu's long fingers in that same place.

"Did you make love to her?" I whispered. I didn't have to speak her name.

"Once," he said.

I groaned.

"Stop," he said. "It is only one of the things of life. It wasn't about anything much. The moment was there, that's all."

He slept. Having failed his family's tests of goodness, had he been my aunt's good child? He had left home without a plan in his head. He was waiting for the plan of war to shape his life.

He stirred, awoke.

"Did I sleep for a long time?"

" 'I be here so long without your comfort.' "

"What's that?"

"It was in the letter you mailed for me, the one the prisoner dropped from the window."

"I'm back now."

He put his hand on my breast. I felt a faint surprise as though it were not possible we were there together in his bed. He had not asked me what meaning I chose to find in the prisoner's words. He was simpler than I had imagined.

Nina had stayed in the operating room for nearly two hours. Sam told his surgeon friend she was a medical student. She was given a cotton mask and a stool to stand on so she wouldn't miss anything. The patient had many obstructions in his intestinal tract.

"The doctors talked and joked during the operation. I almost passed out when the surgeon made the first long incisions in the man's belly, and his guts ballooned out softly like an aquatic plant in the sea. I told myself it was beautiful. But I was terrified; then the terror went away. I had to leave before it was over because the ether was making me sick. Sam was surprised I stayed as long as I did."

"Was the man all right?"

"No. He died that night."

"I couldn't watch such a thing."

"Sam said doctors leave things inside a patient sometimes, pieces of gauze or cotton, when they know someone is going to die. It's a favor they can do for a person."

"They kill them?"

"If they know they can't live."

"How can they be sure?"

"You're asking too much."

"But you have to be sure a doctor isn't going to kill you when you have to have an operation!"

"I meant—you're asking too much about anyone being sure of anything. There's hope, that's all."

"Nina! You haven't thought about it!"

"It's true. My mind floats away when I try to concentrate on it, on what I saw. I'm ashamed of the way I do what's right in front of me, and take what's offered."

"The way you went off with Sam?"

"I guess so."

"I went to bed with Len," I said, sounding oddly stubborn to myself, but what about?

"Poor Lulu," Nina said. "We've stolen away all her men."

"Not Mr. Metcalf," I said. We both laughed. Later I thought about what she had said. She had had the same thought about Len I had had, Len and Lulu, but hadn't mentioned it.

CHAPTER

NINE

Sam took Nina to a grand restaurant. She was reluctant to go. She was bothered by the thought that she would have not only to eat what he ordered for her but show reverence for it. And she didn't have the right clothes. But what oppressed her most was her conviction that the evening was to mark the end of their affair.

"I'm not suffering. Does he think if I were, such a thing would solace me? It's dreadful, so mortifying, to be paid off with a meal! But I'll go. Because it is the end. The more he spends, the less obligation he'll feel. And later, he'll forget so quickly that when he sees me again, I'll be someone he knows slightly. And so it will not only be over, it will be as if it never happened. How to arrive unwrinkled at the grave . . ."

He dropped her off at Gerald's. He had to return to Fort Benning. She arrived looking pale and tired, but within an hour color had returned to her cheeks. "I ate too much," she whispered to me. "It was disgusting!"

Len and I were there along with the Lindners. Claude dropped in, too. No one had seen him for over a week except Nina, and she had had only fleeting glimpses of him.

Marlene was wearing a gypsy blouse embroidered with coarse operatic roses that showed off her plump chalky shoulders. She was sulking. Norman was delivering a sermon on color during which his eyes grew moist as though he were about to cry. I knew he regarded himself as having an artist's superior sensitivity to the visible world. Was he also sentimental about color? He spoke excitably and with a touch of truculence. He paused to draw breath. Gerald asked Nina what she had eaten at Arnaud's.

"How did you know I was there?"

Gerald looked slightly disconcerted. "Sam said something about it, taking you there."

"He made an announcement?" Nina asked dryly.

Marlene said loudly, "Nina, your feet will grow and spread and get as big as Greta Garbo's if you don't stop wearing those Mexican sandals."

Claude had just arrived. "Like Garbo, Nina doesn't need to waste a moment's concern about her feet. They are beautiful because she doesn't attempt to stuff them into a size that's twice too small," he said.

Marlene looked cowed. She said awful things about Claude behind his back, but in his presence she tried to attract his interest, speaking to him with a trace of an English accent as though it were a token of higher cultivation.

The Lindners became morose and silent. Claude walked to where Nina was sitting and stood behind her chair. I went back to gazing at Len, who was smoking a cigarette, his hair a gauzy dazzle in the shadowy corner where he sat. His presence in a room took all my attention. I studied him like a lesson.

Across Gerald's lap was a folded newspaper whose edges he had been curling and uncurling during Norman's lecture. He asked us if we'd seen the headlines. The Germans had attacked Russia from the Arctic all the way to the Black Sea. Norman started forward.

"The Soviet Union was buying time. Didn't I always say so? Stalin knew this would happen!"

"How foolish you are, Norman," Claude said dispassionately. "You believe in life as geometry. You place your tiny grid on the world and erase all that doesn't fit in. What doesn't fit in is life itself."

Norman bounced up from his chair, his mouth open, but before he could speak, Claude bowed slightly to Gerald and Catherine and said he must go, to please excuse him. Nina got up, too, and said she would leave with him.

"How dare he!" Marlene cried, half hoping, I suspected, that Claude would hear her as he went down the steps to the sidewalk. "A pervert telling us about life!"

I was surprised when Norman told her to pipe down. "We don't name-call," he said primly.

"People everywhere are sitting in rooms and talking like we are, and soon we'll go to sleep as they will, and this black wall of death is coming," Catherine said.

I looked at the window that faced the porch and the dim

street beyond. The light of a street lamp picked out streaks and whorls of dust on the glass like storm clouds frozen in the sky.

"It's all the government's fault," Norman said.

"I want to be in it," Len spoke up suddenly. "I want to fight them."

The Lindners said they had to go. Marlene looked at Len. "Coming?" she asked him. She turned to smile at me in a way she must have imagined was girlish. It was triumphant. Everyone knew Len and I were lovers now. After all, I was a member of a group. The thought of it made me laugh. We knew much about each other, nearly as much as we didn't know; we sensed the first faint stirrings of change, of crisis, long before we found words for it, as though, clumsy as we were, we were equipped with long delicate feelers. Lately we had begun to speak differently about Claude. I heard in all our voices, in the things we said, a heightened awareness that perilous elements were gathering force at the core of his hidden life—which, in truth, was never truly hidden except in the sense that the ultimate being of another person is always, unavailingly, hidden.

Nina saw him more than any of us, of course, and when we saw her, we looked to her as a messenger from another country. "He's fine," she would say. So far—I would think.

After the Lindners had gone, Len and I stood up to go. I never brought him to my bed in the little room over the kitchen.

"It was so unlike Claude to go at the Lindners like that," Catherine said. "Not that I minded. She can be so mean. We let her get away with it because Gerald feels sorry for her. You do, don't you, Gerald?"

"Not at the moment," Gerald said. "It wasn't our best evening. Never mind. I think we ought to take that trip down the
delta. Helen, see if Nina can come. We can all fit into the old tin
lizzie."

We agreed on the following Saturday, and Len and I left.

On the street I put my arm around his waist and held him to
me for a moment. "Let's run home," he said. We both turned at
the same instant to look back at the house. Was he thinking, I
wondered, of Catherine's words? Of that black wall of death?

Nina had come to visit me in my room. "I love it here," she said.
"It feels so *safe*."

We were speaking about Claude, and she had broken off to
look at each sweet thing in the room, smiling.

"What sort of family does he have? Where are they? Can you
see him as a child?"

"He has cousins. His mother's sister's children. They are
older than he is. He hardly ever sees them, though they live in
the city—not in the Quarter. He has to go to a business meeting every so often, about the store."

"Is his aunt alive?"

"No. They're all dead, his parents, his aunt. There are distant
family connections in France. When he went there, he visited
them in a place called Blois. They were polite."

"He's the only child."

"Yes. He loves France. He says you can't have it the way you
can have Italy. The French say—Look! How beautiful our
country is! But they won't let you in. You can look, that's all."

"Norman says it's the light there that made the painters so
great."

"I've heard him say that, since he says everything a thousand times. He hasn't been to France anyhow. What Claude says is that it's what the light falls on that is so different."

"Are you . . . attracted to him?"

"Oh, my Lord, no! There's something in the center of your soul that says *no*." She ran her hands over the coverlet. "I love him," she said gravely. "It's a strong love but without heat. Cool, rather, pale blue like the sky when you sense the immense distance of everything. Sometimes it's as if he's the guest in his own house, not me. And sometimes it's as if he were a very young grandfather, almost as young as I am and with enormous concerns of his own."

"He watches over you."

"Yes. Did I tell you Sam came by to see me? He told me about some nurse he's started to sleep with—that awful way men do, as if you were only a bystander. He makes me feel false; he seems to assume that now he can behave as though I were a pal. Claude understands all that, but he doesn't ever tell me what to do. He has a way of listening. It's so intent that it's far better than advice. He doesn't believe in advice anyhow, because people do what they want to in the long run."

"Have you seen that boy ever? The Italian boy?"

"I saw him once, I'm almost sure. I got up in the night. The light was on in the living room. The big fan was turning. I think it was the sound of it that woke me. A young dark-haired man was sitting in a chair, crying. Claude was standing close to him, holding his hand tightly."

"Did you ever find out what he drinks when he makes the libation to the gods?"

"Only one god. David and I think it's absinthe. You can't buy it anywhere . . . it's illegal to sell it in this country, but I expect the young man brings it to him. Those people, his family, they can get anything, especially if it *is* illegal. Claude showed me a picture of a painting, a woman sitting by herself at a table, drinking absinthe. I think the painter is Degas."

"You're going to school."

"The University of Claude de la Fontaine. But it isn't all school." She laughed and touched my hand. "Don't look so serious," she said. "Often we speak of daily things, call to each other from different rooms, eat sandwiches standing up, gossip."

"I was thinking about something bad happening to him."

"It's hardly ever out of my mind. He does everything so well—but he can't manage that. He can't stop."

She looked at me for a long moment. "I didn't feel much when it was over with Sam. It wasn't hard to stop. I don't know which is worse."

Gerald sang a song about the Titanic:

> Ain't it a shame 'bout the Titanic goin' down!
> Churrin and wives—ever'body lost their lives!
> Ain't it a shame 'bout the Titanic goin' down . . .

We traveled a narrow road, and the grass grew so tall on either side the road always seemed to be about to give out, to dwindle down to nothing amid the rampant green growth. Though the day was windless, the trees, laden with Spanish moss, appeared to be fleeing north. "Prevailing wind," said Gerald. He stopped the car once and we sat in the sultry silence. Across a wild meadow, raised on thick stone posts, was an abandoned plantation house; its wood was the color of ashes. The windows were broken, empty of light or movement. The house had a staring, aggrieved look. One of its huge doors was ajar. Runners of snakelike plants grew all about the walls, coiling through windows, circling about the thick columns. The wilderness was taking it into itself as a net takes a great fish.

"The Old South," Gerald said softly.

"Ghosts . . . a place for ghosts," Catherine murmured.

Len said, "It's the way I imagined the south. Not just old, but close to ancient."

"Why does it sit up so high?" Nina asked.

"Because of the floods that come along," Gerald replied. "This land is mostly water. A Cajun has his pirogue nearby all the time, ready for the change that can come so quick, not from the sky, from the river."

Lonville was a hamlet of a few shacks, a bumpy dirt road, a spindly wharf that walked on rough-hewn posts out of a mangrove swamp to the river. At its farther end stood a tiny shack with a dim blue light in its window. It was a place where the village men could drink and talk, a social place. The owner's wife cooked, and Gerald was taking us there for supper.

Gerald's house was a shack, too. An outhouse stood in the back. Inside the house it was cool and damp. Catherine made a fire in a squat black stove that stood in the middle of the one room. There was a low persistent hum, like several simmering kettles. "The bees," she said.

We drank tea sitting around the stove. Beyond the open window, the little noise of spoons in cups, the humming of the bees in the wall, there seemed to exist a vast enigmatic stillness. That afternoon we did not speak of the war in Europe, although now I read the newspaper every day. As the Russian cities fell, as the German army rolled toward Leningrad, I felt Len was being pulled away from me ineluctably.

Instead, Gerald told village stories. At some moment Catherine beckoned me to the window. She was holding a box of faded tintypes she had found in the house in an old trunk. As she held one out to me, of a plump woman with frizzed hair in a striped high-collared jacket, two middle-aged men passed by, their faces and heavy shoulders framed briefly by the window. I heard the syrupy sputter of their voices.

"They're talking Cajun," she said. She looked up from the box straight at me and took the tintype from my hand. "Those are two of the three men who hurt Gerald," she said so softly I thought I'd imagined she'd spoken.

My throat closed up as though someone had taken hold of it. When I felt I could speak, I said, "They should be in jail."

"He wouldn't press charges. And some other folk from around here rescued him—he would have died if they hadn't found him and got him to a hospital. It was heroic of them. They hate and fear anything to do with the city. He told the doctor it was unknown assailants."

Later, as we walked to the wharf to have supper, I walked alongside Gerald. It was hard to ask him what I wanted to ask, but I hadn't been able to think of anything else since Catherine had pointed out the two men.

He answered so quickly, he must have guessed what was on my mind. Perhaps he had seen me seeing them.

"I don't know why nothing happened to them. It was like a lynching," I said.

"No, it wasn't," he said. "They weren't out to kill me. And I wasn't innocent. I celebrated the life here, but they saw it as my using them. They didn't have any idea about the harm they were going to do me——that I was going to be so sick. It was a moonless night, so dark, and they'd been drinking a lot. You see, it might even have been a mistake."

"A mistake!"

"They could have thought I was someone else they had a grudge against. Then, when they knew it was me there in the dark, they could have recollected they'd heard something . . . that I'd told some secrets about them."

"Do you talk to them?"

"Jesus, no!" he burst out. "Sometimes I want to kill them!"

In the dark little hole of a shack with the blue light in the window, we crowded together in one of the two booths and ate crabs and shrimp and rice and drank warm beer. If one of us moved or reached for salt, we all had to shift about. The physical constriction of it was oddly comforting.

On the ride back to New Orleans, Gerald paused so we could once again see the deserted plantation house, this time by the light of the full moon. Its windows gaped like burnt hungry mouths. What the moonlight didn't touch bulked hugely, heavy, black, eerie. The chimneys were like demonic ears. A little further on, a car as old as Gerald's but battered as though with sledgehammers appeared suddenly in front of us after it turned out of a dirt track, and began to weave from side to side of the road. Gerald gripped the steering wheel. We all bent for-

ward tensely. "Dead drunk . . . the son of a bitch," he muttered.

It felt like an hour before Gerald was able to turn the car,
with a violent lurching, onto the hummocky shoulder and pass
the other car. The driver hit his horn again and again, a thin
plaintive honk that accompanied us for a mile or so before it
was absorbed by the night.

"I guess he wanted company," Gerald said.

"Another hairbreadth escape," said Catherine.

A note with my first name written on it was driven into the
mesh of the screen door with an open safety pin. I unfolded the
lined paper and read it to the others who had crowded around
me. We had just gotten home from Lonville. It was very late.
The note said: "Lulu is in Charity Hospital. She fell and cracked
her head." It was signed *J. Charles.*

Nina and Len went with me. On the way, Len told us that J.
Charles was an elderly man who lived in the room next to Lulu's. Apart from that, we didn't speak as we hurried through
the silent empty streets.

"She's a handful and a half," the nurse said to us coldly. She
seemed to be the only person around in the dimly lit hall. "The
niece comes with me, you-all wait here."

"Is she all right?" Nina asked anxiously.

"As all right as she can be," the nurse replied. "I can tell you
she wasn't feeling much pain. She's sobered up now. All she got
was a hard bang on the head."

In the women's ward, at the farthest end from the door and

surrounded by empty beds, Aunt Lulu was sitting up staring into the darkness.

"We had to stick her off there by herself, she was making such a racket," the nurse said. A small light was clamped to the iron headbar of her bed. It shone on her freckled arms and her big hands folded in her lap. She turned her head very slowly as we approached. "It was the goddamned plank," she said to me as she fingered the bandage that partly covered her head.

The nurse said, "You can stay a few minutes. Keep your voices down. There are sick people sleeping here. Then you'd better talk to the resident."

As the nurse left us, Aunt Lulu said, "Someone must have taken it away from the stairs. And, naturally, I expected it to be there and, of course, I fell into that goddamned branch of the Mississippi and got soaked. If it hadn't been for J. Charles, I think I'd have drowned. Can you take me home now?"

She gazed up at me. Her face was bare of makeup, scrubbed so clean I wondered if a nurse had wanted to remove more than powder and rouge. She half lifted herself up from the pillow and strained toward me, her expression full of entreaty. "Could you?" she whispered. I clasped her hand in mine, and she brought my hand up to her face and pressed dry lips against my knuckles. It was the first time she had touched me in such a way. I felt the weight of her person and her trouble as if for the first time, too. "I'll talk to the doctor," I said. "I'll get you out of here."

The resident was a tall skinny man, sooty-eyed with fatigue. He bit at the cuticles of his nails as he spoke to me. The blow to her head was not serious, he said. Drunks are always falling down. But her liver was enlarged. If she didn't quit drinking, she'd be dead in a year. His voice was quick, sharp, impersonal, his words like sparks struck off flint. He said I could take her home and she should spend a few days in bed.

He sighed hugely. "You heard what I said, didn't you? People tend not to hear doctors." He spoke wearily but not unkindly. "She has nearly completed her own ruin. She really ought to be in a drying-out tank."

"I'll do what I can," I replied, without a glimmer of an idea of what I could do.

Len found a late-cruising taxicab and Nina had enough money to pay the fare. The ballroom was a shambles, utensils flung far from the kitchen, clothes strewn everywhere, the balcony windows open.

I got her into bed while Len and Nina straightened the room as best they could. My aunt lay beneath the sheet fighting sleep. Each time her lids closed, she forced them open. A faint smile lingered about her lips as she murmured, "I'm so glad . . . oh, so glad . . ."

I told Len and Nina I would stay the night and they left. The next morning, I used the telephone at Murphy's bar to say I wouldn't be in that day, my aunt was ill. There was an earthen beery smell in the bar and the sour stale smell of the much-used mop an elderly colored man was passing over the floor. I went to a bakery and bought small sweet buns, and then I returned to the ballroom and made coffee on the hot plate.

Although she was weak, she ate all the buns and drank the

last drop of coffee. I gave her one of the pills the resident had given me to ease her headache. As the day wore on, she grew stronger. By late afternoon, she was walking around the room in her old green dressing gown. I had not thought of Len all day. I had not thought of much except Lulu. I was overwhelmed with a desire to serve her. I felt solemn with selflessness, recognizing it to be an uncommon state of feeling. Its purity was marred, of course, by my consciousness of it.

"Is there something going on between Nina and Len?" she asked me as dusk came with its long shadows.

"Oh—why no!" I exclaimed. She stared at me silently.

"It's Len and me," I said bravely. I felt that day I must only say what was so.

She plucked at the bandage on her head. It was half-unwound, hanging about her ears in loops. Suddenly she grasped it with both hands and pulled it off. I saw a large blue- and yellow-tinged bruise on her upper forehead. She touched it, wincing.

"Well—it's your life," she said. "I'll say nothing except that I need cigarettes."

"I'll go and get them."

"And beer."

"Aunt Lulu, the doctor told me your liver is enlarged and that you're killing yourself. Please . . ."

"Go get it for me. Samuel Mosby Bridge is my husband and my *doctor*. I shall do as I *please* with my stupid, stupid life! And don't *look* at me like that! You look like a cow! You look like my simpering sister!"

"I won't buy you beer."

"Then J. Charles will, or one of a dozen passersby on the street whom I will pay for the favor."

I went out and bought her cigarettes and beer.

"Don't expect me to thank you," she said with a wry smile as she drew a cigarette from the pack. "But if it's any comfort to you, I appreciate your effort not to contribute to my downfall."

I went back to work the next morning. When I came home from work, Nina was sitting in Gerald's front room. They were out. She looked up at me from where she was sitting on the edge of the chair. Her eyes were wide and staring.

"Lulu is okay," I said. "That is to say, she's on her feet and, by now, drunk."

"Listen!" she said and held up her hand urgently, as though I were about to launch into a speech she must prevent me from making.

"I've been here an hour. I was sent home early. We all were, out at the lake. A test fighter plane crashed today in front of the hangar. It dug a hole in the earth so deep you could only see the tail sticking out. Someone said they had to take out the pilot with spoons."

I sat down, nearly fell down. We were silent, staring at each other. I thought suddenly of the two large men I had seen from the window of Gerald's shack in Lonville. I wondered if they hadn't been a portent of immense changes, the sense of which was flooding me with fear.

CHAPTER

TEN

Miss Beauregard informed me that many of the store customers covered their faces with lotions ordinarily used to prevent bodily perspiration. I noticed their faces and necks, greased and gleaming and smudged with their own fingerprints. I felt nearly smothered during the day; night brought only slight relief. Miss Beauregard made me a gift of a small fan painted with fat blue ribbons against pink clouds, and I used it, walking along the street, as I saw other people do. The air was lifeless, as heavy as wet horse-blankets.

Mother wrote, saying every year until August she forgot, thank heavens, about the humidity of the Hudson Valley, and she hoped I was more comfortable than she was. The character of her letters had been slowly changing. She had less to say about herself and asked more questions about my life. Was I "seeing someone"? I never mentioned friends, she observed.

She hoped I wasn't lonely. Lulu could be "very jolly" if she felt like making the effort. She would miss me at Thanksgiving, but surely I could come home for Christmas, since I would have earned some vacation time from the store by then.

I carried the letter around with me for a week or so, wondering what I could say about Len. I was "seeing" a rabbi's son, and her sister would be dead within a year if she didn't stop drinking. I couldn't write such news to Mother. We did not have the habit of truth.

Colored people never had to be pointed out to me, since their difference was visible. But she always noted that so-and-so was a Jew: the owner of the dry-goods store, a new dentist in town, infrequently, a couple who rented a cabin. "When you hear a name that ends in *stein* or *witz*, you can tell," she had instructed me. She observed that Jews were smart; she hinted that being smart "that way" lacked goodness and dignity. Besides, they had unsavory personal habits she didn't go into.

I neither believed nor disbelieved her. It was the way she was; what she said, her opinions, never struck me as being true in the larger world, only true to her. What I was sure about was that were I to write her about Len, and Lulu's perilous health, she would have set about with more desperate intent than usual to try to find those silver linings of hers.

Yet I missed her physical solidity and vigor, the small comedies I saw in the bustle in which she managed her days, her tasks. I remembered her joke about my setting out from home with my possessions in a kerchief tied to a stick. I hardly knew that humorous side of her. It was mysterious and tantalizing to me, like the glint of a distant light such as I had sometimes seen from my bedroom window at night, embedded in the far hills across the Hudson.

I was harrowed by love. We doubled ourselves and became four people instead of two; two of them talked together in bars, on walks, in the company of others, civil, even formal. There would be a sudden look, a flash between us, a feeling of faintness would come over me, and I would sense the imminence of those other two who sweated and cried out in the damp heavy nights.

"Do you ever think it's grotesque?" I whispered one gray dawn, my lips against his shoulder.

"Yes," he said, "when I think at all."

He sought me out at Gerald's. Often, I found him waiting for me at the employees' door of the store. There were times when he wanted to come with me on Saturdays when I met Nina on the banks of the river. Though I missed him, I said no. I had to spend time with someone else every so often, though our being apart tormented me and increased my longing to be with him.

For all of that, I felt at times an absence in him, empty pauses in the rush of feeling between us.

He spoke of the war; he always told me the news. American soldiers were now in Iceland. "I read the paper, too," I said. "I think of you being taken away by the draft. Don't you know that?" He didn't reply. I wanted him to talk about the future, our future—I couldn't. I stared at couples on the streets as though I might learn something significant from their behavior.

I told Nina I could not bear the thought of being separated from him. I wondered aloud how men and women survived such a parting. "You once said love was a calling," I reminded her.

"I did? I don't recall even thinking that, but maybe I did once. If it's a calling, then crucifixion is bound to result." She smiled at me in a teasing manner that was not like her when we spoke of serious things.

"And Sam? Has he stopped talking to you about his nurse?"

"Yes. I made him stop. When he takes me out to dinner, not to fancy places anymore, he treats me in a doctorly way, advising me about my life, my character."

"Does it make you unhappy?"

"Not especially. But I feel a certain shame."

"Why?"

"I was so indifferent to him. I feel I must put up with his lectures. It's rather comical. He doesn't understand me at all but thinks he does."

It was Sunday and we were in Claude's living room. Above us, a large ceiling fan turned sluggishly. In his garden beyond the French doors, flowers drooped amid the thick glossy greenery.

"Claude took me to a strange party," she said and paused, waiting, I suppose, to see if I was willing to drop the topic of love. I rested my head against the back of the chair.

"It was in an immense apartment somewhere near the Pontalba buildings. A whole floor, room after room, the lampshades amber so that the whole place was the color of honey. And brocade pillows, huge ones, on the floor, if you wanted to sit there.

There must have been about twenty people. The hostess was tall and gaunt like a scarecrow. She had on a purple chiffon gown and gold slippers. They weren't like the people we know. Much older and very formal."

I was looking at a small tree in Claude's garden, a flowering tree of some sort, with an intricate lacing of branches which suggested to me all that is hidden in a human body, passages that endlessly connect and carry the fluids of life.

Straining toward the months, the years, that lay ahead, I feared I was losing the ground of the present, losing balance. All by myself, without a word to Len, I was concocting a life with him in imaginary time. When I looked at his face, full of private reflection, I felt a particular loneliness I'd never felt before except when I looked down from my window and saw my father on the day he went away, and knew he was going. I must give up the future, I told myself. Could one do that? Or must there always be this blind frantic tunneling away from the moment?

I looked up at the slow-moving blades of the fan, oars in a puddle of dense moist heat. Nina was still talking. I blinked; her voice was a murmur that seemed to reach me through thick curtains.

"They spoke of books, music, and they don't talk about themselves at all, the way everyone does at Gerald's. Does it ever seem to you that people's faces look deeper somehow, here in the south? Even those people at that party."

"What did you wear?"

"The blue dress. Claude gave me a crepe de chine shawl of his mother's. He draped it around my throat, and I said I felt he was leading me off to be slaughtered. He said he was. New places and new people. It's always a chance, he said. I did make a fool of myself. I thought they were all gossiping about a woman they knew, Madelaine. And I asked where did she live and what did she do? I wanted to say something, to *be* there. And they laughed and laughed. Because it was not a woman— it was a *madeleine*, a little cake that you can dip in tea or coffee, and there is an enormously long novel where the cake is important. The novel is about time. Lost time."

"Time. I was just thinking of that," I said. "I'm forever imagining time to come. Why were they so mean? Why do people laugh just because you don't know something?"

"That's when people laugh the most. I didn't mind, really. Claude told of going to see the grave of the writer of that book when he was in Paris. My face was flushed all the time because I was so excited. Everything was so suave and sleek, the food so good, and lovely drinks, and except when they laughed, their voices were so calm and low. How different everything is! Do you remember how it was in that little shack with the blue light where Gerald took us to supper? If it weren't so hot, I think I'd get up and dance. Thinking about that party makes me restless. I'll never get to see all I want to see. I want to go to Marcel Proust's grave some day—even if I don't read the book. But what are you thinking about? You look so sad!"

"My father. How he had to run away from us when he lost what he most cared about."

I pictured the tack room filled with the light of late afternoon, the calm late summer light that seems to move more slowly at that time of day, and the stalls where those great beautiful beasts shifted from side to side, their heads held so stiffly as though they wore helmets, and how alertly they turned toward us when he and I took them a pail of oats for a treat.

"My grandfather believed in reason above all else," Nina said. "He told me once when he was peeling an apple for me to eat that he would teach me how to do it the way he did, so that the whole skin fell off in a circular strip. It was simply a matter of looking at the apple, studying it, thinking about it, he said. There were terrible governments and wars because people used their wills in the wrong direction. He said we were all wild children, the whole human race, and must be instructed in how to think."

"But by what? Whom?"

"He never told me that."

"Can you peel an apple that way?"

"It's only a trick." She sighed and glanced at the ceiling. "I suppose the fan does some good. I feel like a lizard glued to a rock. So *stopped*. I wish I could be overtaken, wake up one morning and find myself passionately interested in something— becoming a doctor or a golfer . . . "

"Why not both?"

"No, really! I would plan in a serious, determined way how to bring it about, in the way my grandfather peeled the apple. I want to be overtaken by love, too, so that I'm in it, drowned in it, without thoughts."

"What is that book called? The one about time?"

"*Remembrance of Things Past*. But Claude says it should be called *In Search of Lost Time*. That's what it means in French."

"*Remembrance* makes me think of church," I said.

She nodded. "It's like a bell tolling. I found out that there's another meaning to *madeleine*—a remorseful prostitute." She laughed lightly. "A rueful whore," she said.

"You've been overtaken by Claude," I said. I was sorry for the resentment in my voice. She had heard it, too.

"I know. I talk about him so much, it must drive you crazy."

"You have such a good time with him."

"Yes. He's taken me to jazz clubs. Sometimes David Hamilton comes by and plays for us, Schubert mostly. He's so serious about music, but so silly about other things. And I have to be careful with him. I love it when he plays, but if I show too much enthusiasm or I get too friendly, he gets stiff, and cold as a fish. I don't see how I'll ever be able to live with anyone else besides Claude. He likes things to be orderly. I'm used to that because grandpa was that way, too. But if I leave things scattered around, or dishes in the living room, Claude doesn't scold. He doesn't think he made the world."

"Is there anything more about the Italian?"

She glanced quickly at the French doors. "David told me there's some businessmen's club where they've begun to talk about it. They'd love a real public scandal because Fountain's would suffer, and it's a much better store than any of their stores."

"But does everyone know about it?"

"I think so, in different ways. Do you know what you truly think about it?"

I thought for a moment. "I guess not. The idea of his being hurt is terrible. I want him to stop seeing that boy so nothing will happen to him."

"I ran into Lulu yesterday," Nina said. "I made a mistake. I thought that after we met her with Mr. Metcalf, she wouldn't be angry with me. But she is. As soon as she saw me, just as I started to say hello, she made some horrible gesture at my neck. Now I'm hexed."

"Lulu can't hex a cockroach."

Like a figure in a dream, dark and shambling, Howard Meade's girlfriend, Olivia, suddenly loomed amid the thick greenery of the garden. She was barefoot and wearing a man's flannel bathrobe. Her hands were outstretched toward the doors as though she'd gone blind.

"Olivia!" exclaimed Nina, getting up and going to let her in.

Olivia staggered past the piano toward where I was sitting. As soon as she saw me, she began to sob loudly. One of her eyes was bruised and nearly shut. Her right foot was bleeding near her ankle.

"Howard," she gasped. "So drunk . . . Can I hide here?" She coughed as though on the verge of retching. Nina put her arm around Olivia's shoulders and, leading her across the room, said, "I'll wash your face and your foot. You've stumbled on something. Come to the bathroom."

"He said I was making eyes at someone!" she wailed. "He was drunk all night and raving and he wouldn't stop saying it, that I was doing something rotten under the table, and he began to hit me. What's happened to me? What shall I do? Is my eye black?"

"First, let me clean you up. Then we'll think about what to do."

"But where's Claude?" Olivia cried. She turned clumsily in a circle. I glimpsed her matronly breasts and tobacco-colored nipples.

"He'll be along soon," Nina said softly.

Olivia seemed to see her for the first time. "I've been drinking," she said sadly. "Oh! Oh! This must be the end of me."

Nina took her to the bathroom, and I went into the kitchen thinking I must do something, make coffee, something.

She was half Meade's age, a pretty plump girl with narrow eyes, something Oriental about them. I had seen her once walking a step or two behind him as they went down the street, like an Oriental wife, pausing when he paused.

Claude came in so quietly I didn't hear him until he was standing beside me as I looked at the cabinets, wondering where the coffee was, uneasy about trespassing.

"Can I help?" he asked.

"Oh, Claude! Olivia is here, in the bathroom with Nina. Howard has beaten her up. She needs a place to hide out."

"He'll track her down," he said. So fleetingly, I wasn't sure I'd seen it, a look of intense apprehension crossed his face. He picked up an oyster knife that lay on the counter and examined it, running his finger along the stubby blade. When he put it down, he smiled somberly at me. "First comes the word, then a shove, then a slap and then a fist is doubled up. They both know it will happen. It's not the first time. Why do you suppose they let it happen?" He was looking into my face. Suddenly he laughed. "You look as though you'd seen a human being. Ghosts aren't so scary."

The child's word, his confiding laugh, were so unexpected, I allowed myself to stare at him. For that brief moment in his kitchen, I was not burdened with a customary way of seeing him. It was as though I were meeting him for the first time.

"She won't want coffee, I think," he said. "Let's go and see what's to be done."

Olivia was sitting in a chair beneath the fan. Her hair was pushed behind her ears. A scarf of Nina's I recognized was tied about the bathrobe. She still looked dazed, but her face was washed and there was a piece of gauze wound around her ankle. She started up upon seeing Claude. "I'm sorry," she said tremulously. "I didn't know where to go."

"You ought to leave him," he said quietly. "You really know that. So there's no more to be said about it. People can defend themselves after all, even if they can't defend life itself."

"Don't lecture me," she said miserably.

"I won't. You can stay here and sleep on the couch. But you know he'll find you. Would you like tea? Or a drink?"

"Oh, God! A drink!" she said brokenly. "Not that! Well, maybe that . . . "

It was at that moment that I heard wild howls from the walk between a high stone wall and the side of Claude's house that led to the garden and the doors. In a few seconds, Howard staggered into the garden, waving his arms in the air as he trampled flowers and shrubbery. He wore a vest but no shirt, and I saw the slack flesh of his upper arms as white as milk. He wore shoes but no socks.

"Olivia! Olivia!" he shouted. He fumbled at the doors, his mouth working spasmodically as he pushed and banged and kicked and finally stumbled across the threshold. Nina and Olivia had fled the room. Howard crashed into the piano, recoiled, and saw Claude.

"Where is she!" he cried.

"No one will tell you the time of day when you're in such a state," Claude said evenly.

Howard's hair was on end; his eyes bulged. He seemed to be trying to make himself taller. "Don't *you* tell me anything, delta queen! You with your dirty boys' club! The whole world knows about you! You think because you've got a girl living here——"

"You're in my house," Claude said icily. "Now you can get out of it!"

Nina reappeared, running to stand next to Claude. Howard did not seem to notice her. "You'll get yours, Madame Pompadour," he said with an ogre's mad grin. "And I'll dance and sing the day you do."

He suddenly raised his hands, formed them into fists and gave a great groaning shout. Olivia, her head down, was padding by me in a cloud of scent. She must have poured all of Claude's cologne over herself.

"You unspeakable fat bitch!" Howard shouted, running at her. As he shot a fist toward her, Nina stepped between them and caught the blow on her cheek. She staggered and fell to her knees.

Meade grunted and swayed. "A mistake," he mumbled. Claude helped Nina to stand. I put my arms around her and she laid her head on my shoulder; she was breathing rapidly, brokenly. Claude stood in front of us, holding his arms straight out.

There was no further attack. As I shifted Nina's weight slightly—I was off balance—Howard and Olivia went into the garden, where a moment later I saw them embrace, his long thin arms clutching her to himself like a spider embraces its web-bound prey. I heard rending sobs and sounds that were nearly words as, holding on to each other, they disappeared from view.

"Nina?" Claude called softly.

She lifted her head from my shoulder, took a step away from me. There was a dark red mark on her cheek. I started to touch it. "No!" she ordered me. "Let it be."

"I'll get you a drink," Claude said.

"No. No. I don't want a drink. I don't want anything."

"Shall we go for a walk?" he offered. "We can go to the square. You'll come back to yourself. It's quiet there."

"I've never been hit before."

A bird called from the garden. The fan whispered above us.

"You must not suffer so much," Claude said. He began to cry silently.

"Don't cry for me," Nina said, turning to him. Slowly, with visible effort, she reached out her hand to touch his arm very lightly, as though to touch anyone at all was nearly beyond her at that moment.

I was with Nina in a café on Bourbon Street a few days later when Howard Meade apologized to her. I saw him standing at the entrance, peering about. He was fully dressed in one of the dark business suits he always wore, and his face hung over the rest of him like a dim lamp. I thought him sober if only because he appeared so hesitant and elderly. Drunk, there was always a quality of excitement about him, blurred and incomprehensible, but one that imparted to him a kind of mimed energy. He was slack now, a suit of clothes, an elderly face.

"Howard Meade," I said to Nina in an undertone.

I heard her sharp intake of breath. By then he had seen us and was coming to us.

"I'm absolutely horrified," he said to Nina. "What I did was beyond the pale. Will you forgive me? Can you?"

She was staring down at the table. Her hands gripped its edge.

"Please. Look at me," begged Howard. He had spoken in a low voice, but several customers were watching our booth, though his large body hid us from their eyes.

Nina slowly lifted her head and looked at him.

"Oh dear, oh dear," he said, seeming on the point of tears. "How I've frightened you!"

"It's all right," Nina said, her lips barely moving. "Would you go away now?"

He had the choked look of someone whose mouth was stuffed with words he was not allowed to speak. His embarrassment was so extreme, I felt myself pulled into it. My face was hot. I could barely draw breath.

"I was not myself," he said piteously.

"But you were!" Nina said.

"Yes . . . yes. That's true. But I'm myself now, too. I haven't had one drink since that day. Won't you say you forgive me?"

"I forgive you," she said tonelessly.

"I'll leave you then," he said. "Thank you for your magnanimity." He shambled out onto the sidewalk, looking back once in a puzzled way as though he had forgotten something but wasn't sure of what it might be.

"Awful, awful . . . " she murmured.

"He knows what he did—at least."

"He won't remember for long."

"He's old. She's only a girl. The thought that she'll leave him one day must drive him crazy."

"No!" Nina declared. "People like that only imitate being human. They have hearts of ice. By now, he's found a bar and gone back to his life's work. Everything except drinking is a display, to keep people from throwing him into a coffin and burying him. Yes, drunks have heard of human feeling . . ."

She was like steel. She held judgments harder than I could have imagined. I had thought of her as Claude's ward. I wondered now as I gazed at her face, so collected and intent with thought, if I had got it all wrong, that it was she who guarded Claude.

CHAPTER

ELEVEN

My childhood, like Nina's and Len's, belonged to an in-between time. The people we knew in New Orleans had been alive during the Great War. We admitted to each other that there were times when we felt like children among the others, and there were evenings at Gerald's when the three of us laughed often and immoderately; we felt a faint sense of being in league against grown-ups.

Away from the company of those grown-ups, there were other, contrary sentiments, lurking and shadowy, within the affection I bore them. I saw much but was only beginning, I think, to understand the opposing elements in them, and there were bleak moments when I did not forgive them for preventing me from loving them entirely.

Because he was the least familiar to me, my feeling toward Claude was more consistent. But I suspected my sympathy for

him was shallower, too, although I had begun to see how rending the division was between his public self and a self that was
not merely hidden but unacknowledged.

Catherine and Gerald's meeting and his discovery of a voca-
tion had come so late; he was in his forties with a whole other
life behind him. His impartiality that I so revered seemed, at
times, to be only aloofness, an inhuman distancing of himself
from ordinary concerns. Was his not seeking retaliation against
his assailants a kind of sublime contempt? Did Catherine *mean*
to make me feel her secretiveness so that I would long to tres-
pass against it? Did she sometimes play at the part of a nearly
tragic, nearly holy late-discovered love?

Sara Bridge was feckless, self-indulgent, softly reaching out
to take what he wanted, softly relinquishing it, impervious to
self-doubt.

As autumn came, the tempo of the days seemed to quicken,
to push on, to pile up like the debris of a flood tide against the
brink of a new war. Up north in my mother's house, I had imagined myself standing in time, immobile like a stone in a stream.
I had been unaware that I was being tumbled along with the
current.

The romantic horror I felt at the idea of being parted from
Len gave way to bewilderment. What would I be parted from
when he was drafted? As he often said, he was waiting. I had
been in the waiting place with him. In that place, formed by a
constant awareness of what was only being postponed, a
change was taking place.

"Don't you know what the Star of David is?" he asked me. I
shook my head. He spoke rapidly, his words running together.

"It's a symbol of Judaism. In the Middle Ages, it was called Solomon's Seal."

"Wait, you're talking too fast!" I protested. But that was not what stung me. It was his impatience.

He repeated what he had said with grim, march-cadenced precision. "The Nazis have ordered all Jews to wear the Star sewn to their clothing. *Jew* is to be written across it." He stared at me deeply—all the way, I felt, to what his look implied was my sparsely furnished gentile soul.

"Why are you talking to me this way? What have I done?" I cried.

He blinked. His head sank to my shoulder. "Nothing," he said. "You've done nothing but . . . oh, God." And then he whispered, "They've encircled Leningrad—to starve them."

I cradled his elbow in my hand. For a moment I took it all in, his words, our vulnerable bodies, naked not in love-making but in death-making. A crack in the earth seemed to have opened, revealing at its center a turbulent, inhuman boiling.

I had trouble sleeping. I awoke in the middle of the night and went downstairs and out into the tangled fragrant garden, hoping Catherine or Gerald would wake up, too, and come and walk with me, comfort me.

Sam Bridge's army leaves grew rare. When he was in New Orleans, he visited only my aunt; I could not think why. Catherine had taken on extra typing work with colleagues of Professor Graves to earn money so that Gerald could accept some of the invitations he received to give readings of his poems.

Nina didn't see the young Italian again at Claude's house, and

Claude was hardly ever there. She and I saw more of each other than we ever had.

We both loved movies and went when we had the money to pay for tickets. "It's the one time you can stare at people as much as you want to without frightening them," she said.

I didn't think of movies in that light. Perhaps I didn't think of actors as "other people," but rather as figures in dreams. For me a darkened theater was a place where I forgot about time. If a man took me, the story of the movie was like a conversation between the two of us for which I had no responsibility. At least, it had been that way with Matthew.

Sometimes I'd catch Nina looking at me as intently as she did at the screen. She couldn't have heard a word I was saying. "I'm not a movie star," I protested once. She laughed apologetically and shook her head and said, "Sorry . . . I was dreaming."

She wasn't dreaming. She was thinking as she studied my nose and skin and hair, drawing, I imagined, some conclusion about me and, like a thief, stealing away with it.

"You've been looking at my hands for hours," I said to her on a Saturday when we were sitting in our usual place on a bank above the Mississippi. I clenched one hand and hid the other in the folds of my skirt. "Have you decided something about them?"

She looked startled and faintly wounded. It was not the first time I'd seen her lost in her musings.

The surface of the river was ridged and gray like the bark of a tree whose name eluded me. Its vast movement south appeared to have been halted, held fast from below to mirror the sky. The air was thick with moisture. I glimpsed a dash of green mold on the heel of my right shoe.

"You have nice large hands, Helen," she said, "but I was really thinking about something else." She touched my knuckles. Where her thin fingers briefly rested, I felt spots of coolness. I didn't much want to ask her what she had been thinking about. I knew she'd tell me. I liked it when she talked about movies—she noticed details that would slip right past me— and clothes, though she didn't have any to speak of and didn't seem interested in them. Although when it came to my clothes, things I bought at a discount at the store, she'd examine them with a serious expression and advise me whether to keep them or not in a courteous, delicate way that touched my heart. It was one of the ways that made up for things about her that drove me crazy.

"This is what was on my mind," she began. She paused and glanced at me as though hoping for a sign. I smiled in response; it must have been an odd smile, a fox grin of opposing feelings—please shut up and go ahead.

"Why do you think people must feel in the right even when it costs them so much? They do and say terrible things and then have such enormous work to make it seem they were right in the beginning and forever."

"Pride."

"But why? Why does pride mean being right? Can't there be pride in truth?"

"Who is to say what that is," I answered as I looked up at the darkening sky. I didn't care about pride, about being right.

I imagined Nina's questions as being part of a list of trials she had set herself, trials with no possible outcome, but whose rigors she'd taken a vow to endure. Among our friends, the questions were accepted as her mark, a special thing like Len's hair or Gerald's gift of mimicry, Claude's linen suits and Catherine's deep husky laugh.

"Everybody says what truth is," Nina went on. "Claude says it's all got to do with monotheism—one god who alone claims all the truth there is."

"Is he still drinking his libations?"

"I don't know. I hardly see him."

"We're going to get caught in the rain," I said, getting to my feet. "I can loan you the money." I had told her earlier as we wandered among the market stalls that *Star Dust*, a new Linda Darnell movie, was playing in a moviehouse on Canal.

She shook her head. "I owe you for the last time we went," she said as she stood. She was still spending part of her pay every week to redeem three of her mother's rings she had pawned when she first came to New Orleans in March, before she found her job.

I thought she had forgotten about the money, and that had made me uneasy, as though the sum were crucial. In a way it was. My pay was barely enough to keep me going—especially with all the clothes I couldn't seem to stop buying.

What I had forgotten was that Nina remembered everything: song titles, entire casts of movies, what people said and what they had worn when they said it, where a chair had stood before it was moved, someone's fleeting gesture and the time of day, the weather, the place where a person had said a thing that interested her.

She was gazing off at the wharves. At anchor alongside them were more merchant ships than I'd seen on the river before. In the leaden light, the motionless ships looked to be under a spell, the seamen all spirited away. Only on the wharf just below us someone moved, a lone colored man who suddenly and violently shoved his hands in his pockets as he stared up at the bridge of a small freighter.

"What's he thinking?" murmured Nina.

I wasn't going to speculate about the thoughts of that colored man, and I said so. She looked at me pensively. "Do you think you're right not to?" she asked with mild inquiry.

"I don't think about it at all. I'm not obliged to," I retorted loudly. She picked up from the ground, where I had left it, the greasy wax paper our sandwiches had been wrapped in and began to fold it neatly. I watched her, feeling wanting, not only in conscience but in tidiness.

"I have enough trouble with my own thoughts," I grumbled.

She laughed. "So you tell yourself!"

"You're awful!"

She looked so meek then, so ready to agree with me, I grabbed her by the shoulders and shook her. "Oh, come on! Let's go to the movies and I'll buy you movie tickets till you get those damned rings out of hock." I glanced back at the river, not intending to at all, and saw the wharf where the colored man had been standing.

"He's gone," she said.

"What do you think he was thinking about?" I asked placatingly.

"Getting away," she said.

"I was only looking at the river because I was trying to recall the name of a certain tree," I said. I heard mulishness in my voice, a victory for her. She touched my hand. "Don't be angry, Helen," she said. Her fingers gripped mine. It was she who led me off the bank. Silently we set off up St. Phillip.

The rain began wildly as we turned onto Royal Street, a torrent of it. We were instantly soaked through. I thought I heard Nina shout. I glanced at her. Her head was bent back, her eyes shut tight, her fair hair turned dark and streaming by the rain. She seemed to be struggling up from beneath water.

The shout had come from elsewhere, perhaps from behind a shuttered window in one of the old houses that stood along the street looming over us, the heavy sag of their walls confined by the black lines of their wrought-iron balconies, and the grilles that covered windows and doors like the tendrils of a powerful vine.

"Nina!" I called out. I was suddenly frightened. She looked like a drowned girl. But I was irritated, too, suspecting I'd caught her in a self-dramatizing pose—especially irritated, I suppose, because among my own imaginings was a picture of myself flinging along the streets of the Quarter in just such a downpour, wearing one of the handsome trench coats—and not much else—I'd seen in the store that would have cost me two months of my pay.

Both of us started to run. People were taking shelter in entranceways or else huddling beneath balconies. A streetcar loomed up alongside us, its bell clanging as it drew to a stop. The whole city felt awash. I grabbed Nina's arm. "In here!" I cried and pulled her into the hall of Aunt Lulu's building. In the open courtyard at our backs, the rain poured down on the stones and the fountain like a torrent of lead pellets. I glanced at Nina. Strands of hair were pasted onto her flushed cheeks. She turned to look down the hall toward the staircase. Was she thinking of that night Sam Bridge had said "Let's drive to Mississippi . . ."?

I stared into the rain; its ferocity made my heart beat fast with a kind of joy. I took a step out of the hall to the sidewalk, which was moving like a shallow river. Nina grabbed my skirt and pulled me back. "You haven't heard a word I've been saying," she said.

"The rain is making too much noise," I said.

"I asked you if you'd noticed the story in the newspaper about the hitchhikers, a boy and a girl who've been killing people."

"No. There's enough terrible news . . ."

"Someone would stop to give them a ride. They'd kill him and drive around in the car until it ran out of gas. Then they would abandon it and look for someone else. They've murdered seven people—two of them women."

A middle-aged waterlogged man stumbled by, his shoes squelching. He blinked at us, looking from Nina to me and back again, choosing.

"How vile!"

"They were caught. Yesterday there was a picture of them in the newspaper. They were grinning—the girl was waving at someone."

"They aren't human."

"But they are! I wonder what they thought about what they did."

"Oh, Nina! People like that—they don't have an inside to think with!"

"But they can make up stories," she said. "Like the girl waving. That was a story. She was pretending she had a friend behind the photographer who was glad to see her even though she'd killed all those people. Even insane people make up stories to prove they're Jesus or royalty. A Black Mass is still a mass."

I recollected what the surface of the river had reminded me of, the bark of the elm trees that grew around the house and stables up north.

"I want to stop feeling the way I do about Len," I said. "Nothing will come of it."

"What is supposed to come of it?"

"Oh—don't stand outside of everything! You know what I mean."

"Marriage."

"Yes. That. The future."

"He doesn't want it?"

"I don't know what he wants."

"You'll have to see, then."

"Sometimes I'm frantic. I want to leave . . . just go . . . not see him again ever."

"People never know how lucky they are," she said sadly. "You don't really want to leave. You want him to think you will."

The rain enclosed us as though we were in a small warm

room. Our heads were close together as we talked and our voices sounded like one voice—a soft birdlike murmuring. I felt a faint derangement, a cloudiness, as though I were feeling the first effects of liquor. The words I had spoken had taken me by surprise. I wanted to take back what I'd said.

Her voice rose urgently. "You're taking too much for granted."

It was because she disliked Len so, that she spoke to me so unquietly.

She took hold of my arm. "Why don't you let him be," she said mildly. "We are mostly alone. You can't always know what's inside another person's head." Her grip suddenly tightened. "Look!" she exclaimed.

Moving toward us in crablike motion, which brought him to the edge of the curb then forced him to swing his body sideways to avoid falling into the street, was Howard Meade. His belly bulged above his dark trousers, preceding the rest of him like some dreadful pet he was obliged to carry with him always. His mouth was agape, his eyes were squeezed shut. He swayed a second, opened his eyes and crossed the street and came to a halt a few feet from where Nina and I stood.

"My God!" Nina breathed. "Let's get out of here!"

Howard Meade looked straight up at the balcony. I pulled Nina against the wall. "He's come to see my aunt," I whispered to her, although it was unlikely he could have heard me in the boom of the rain. He stepped into the entrance and saw us at once.

"Claude," he said in a cracked voice. "Claude," he repeated

then with fussy irritability, as though we were pretending not to understand that one word he had uttered.

Nina gripped his arm. "What? What is it?"

"He's dead. His head was broken. It was smashed. Last night near the Dueling Oaks in the park."

Nina cried out. Her cry rose above the noise of the rain, a slow rise of tearing, grieving sound. She fell against me, and I held her. There was a gust of wind. The rain ceased all at once.

There was an investigation of sorts of the murder. In newspaper stories Claude was referred to as a prominent local business-man. A detective questioned Nina twice. If it hadn't been for his relationship to the store, Gerald guessed that not much at-tention would have been paid to his death. In the end the inves-tigation found that he was killed by a person or persons un-known. Within a week there was nothing further about the murder in the papers.

The detective had pressed Nina about her connection with Claude. Did she pay rent for her room? "He treated me with in-sultingly good manners, so I'd feel like a freak, someone who'd live with a queer. The police knew about the boy. They asked me if I'd ever seen him. I lied. They called him 'little Anthony.' I was braced to lie. And it was easy. I've lived in a dream in that house. I've been outside now, in the police station. The way they looked at me . . . like bloody refuse to be removed from the operating room when the operation is over. It's a pretend investigation. They don't care who killed him—he deserved to die."

For once, Norman Lindner was given the attention he always craved. They were after big fish, he told us at Gerald's a week or so later. The committee that was investigating the criminal activities of the group in Baton Rouge was not going to be sidetracked by a squalid sex crime. Nina reported that the detective had asked her if she'd ever seen any Cubans in Claude's house. "You see?" Norman said triumphantly. "There are more important things at stake here than the life of one man."

I saw Nina look at him, an expression of loathing on her face.

"Anthony, what has happened to him?" she asked me when we were alone. I remembered how the boy had rested his whole length against Claude that evening months ago. "What about Anthony?" she said, crying.

Tom Elder at the store whispered to me that he'd heard that Oriental devices for depraved sexual orgies had been discovered in a trunk in Claude's bedroom.

The only trunks I heard of were three empty ones carried into the house by two colored men under the orders of Claude's cousins, who were eager to fill them up with Claude's treasures. They need not have worried. He had done the conventional thing and left everything to them except the piano, which had been bequeathed to David Hamilton.

David was not questioned by the police, though he waited, ashen-faced and frightened and grieving. He hardly seemed the same man who had insisted to Nina and me that feeling blue was just self-indulgence. He had never had much to do with Claude's friends, but he came to Gerald's often for a while, a waiflike man growing pinched about the nose. The most he would say about the murder was that it wasn't unheard of that men had died for love.

The cousins held a private funeral for Claude, to which none of us was invited.

Claude had not wanted a funeral, he had told David a year earlier. "I can't go up against his relatives," David told Nina. "I'm not so very brave like Claude was. He would have hired a hundred lawyers to stop such a thing if our positions were reversed. Let them do what they want. He's beyond it all. I wish I were."

When he went to oversee the removal of the piano to his apartment, the cousins, who were staying temporarily at Claude's, turned their backs to him and spoke not one word.

Nina was sleeping on a cot again, at the Lindners'. She was grateful to them, she said. But it was hard to sleep. They argued at night in their bed, leaning on their elbows, shouting at each other. "Norman wants Marlene to think exactly as he does— not about personal things, but about Churchill and Roosevelt and Japanese militarism."

Still, they were kind to her, Norman especially, who seemed to acknowledge her misery.

"Claude's goodwill toward me was the blood of life," she said with an intensity that frightened me. I was easily frightened those days.

She was going back north soon, she told me. In a month, she thought. By then she would have saved enough money for train fare with some extra to keep her going while she looked for work in New York City. She wanted to live in the biggest city, where people were strangers to each other. She had her mother's rings back. She could always pawn them or sell them if she needed money.

Two weeks after Claude's death, Len's number came up in the draft lottery. "I think we should get married," he said to me.

I had been living for so many months in an acute state of longing, I was nearly depleted of emotion. Then there was Claude's death, the fact of which I could still hardly take in.

We were going to Chicago. He'd written to his family about me. His mother was very upset. "I hope she'll get over it," he said. "Do you mind terribly being thought of as a disaster for a while?"

No, I didn't mind. I was too sad to mind. And too flat, a flatness of feeling I recalled experiencing as a child when I finally attained something I had been mad with desire for.

My mother wrote in response to my letter with the news: "Hello! My married daughter! Of course it's wonderful! And I'm sure he's very smart and will provide for you. It's too bad he's going to have to be a soldier boy, but the time will pass so quickly!"

I went to see Aunt Lulu to tell her about Len and me.

"Unforeseen results," she said to me gruffly. "Life is strange. Well, I hope you'll be happy. The ancients said that since we can't attain happiness, we might as well be happy without it." She laughed briefly. She rose and went to the hot plate, looked at it meditatively and then returned to the chair she'd been sitting in.

"Why?" she asked. "He's a nice enough boy. But still—why?"

What in her life, I wondered, in her history, made her think she had a right to ask me such a question, with its belittling "nice enough boy"? The effort not to visualize Len in her bed, in her flesh, made my throat ache and my eyes burn.

She was watching me intently now. For an instant I felt like an animal's prey. The urge to flee was powerful. Then, as though a calming hand had touched my face and my head, the anger and fear drained away. I told her about finding the prisoner's letter on the street when I first walked in the Quarter, and reading it. I heard the composure in my voice. I was surprised, and nearly lost it, lost whatever it was that I had gained and didn't know a name for.

"I showed the letter to Len. He gave me a stamp and he mailed it for me. He didn't question my curiosity, or my wanting it to be mailed, even if it didn't ever reach the woman it had been written to. Julette. I think that was her name."

I fell silent. Lulu was looking up at the painted constellations. I heard our breathing. It was almost in unison. "There was sympathy in that," I said. "Something kindly. I don't know how to explain it."

She dropped her gaze and smiled faintly in my direction.

"Well, I suppose that's as good a reason as any," she said.

"Do you want something? Coffee?" I asked.

"No. I was thinking of Claude. The thought of him makes me have to move from one place to another. It's a collar of stone. Poor, poor Claude. The effort of his life, and then . . . Oh, God!

The more I know about myself, the less confidence I have in life."

"Do you think you'll ever go north? To Mother?"

"To Mother," she repeated mockingly. "When I'm too weak to do anything else, I might. The moment has not yet arrived, dear."

She closed her eyes and rested her head against the back of the chair. She had changed. I hadn't been aware of it until then. She was thin, even stringy. Her skin had coarsened and looked pitted. Her hair still blazed, but it was like a dying flame in a gutted house.

I kissed her forehead before I was even conscious of the impulse that had made me bend over her. For a second, her arms went around me. "Be a good girl," she murmured. I straightened up and looked at her. Her eyes were wide open, filled with tears. "Get out," she said gently.

My bags were packed, the old one of my father's and a new valise Catherine had given me. Gerald was going to drive Len and me to the station.

On the morning of the day I went away, I found Gerald at his table in his workroom, gazing down at a piece of paper on which he'd just written something, lifting his pencil as I went to stand beside him.

"Can I see?"

He nodded. "It's nothing I wrote. It's from the end of *Don Quixote*," he said. "It's something Sancho Panza says. I'm going to put it in my notebook."

I had not read *Don Quixote*. I didn't know who Sancho Panza was. I picked up the paper and read:

"Don't die, Don Quixote, don't die. For to die without good reason is the greatest guilt of this life."

I began to weep. Catherine came into the room. The three of us stood together, our arms around each other, until it was time to go.

Over the years, gradually, like birds quieting as the dark advances, their twittering like crystal drops, gradually muting in a long summer twilight, the voices I had come to know so deeply faded away.

Aunt Lulu had a stroke and, at last too weak to do anything else, allowed my mother to come and take her home to the north and nurse her until she died four months later.

Gerald had given two readings, one in Atlanta and one in Charlottesville. When he came home, he went to the hospital. He had bacterial endocarditis. There was no cure for it then, although a few months later a drug was developed that might have saved his life. His wife agreed to a divorce at last, and three days before he died, Catherine and he were married as he lay on his hospital bed.

Sam Bridge was sent to North Africa and was killed during the American invasion of Algeria in 1942.

Norman and Marlene Lindner were divorced a few years after the end of the war.

I ran into her at Rockefeller Center in the early winter of 1952. I had taken my daughter, Lydia, to watch the ice skaters. A heavy woman in expensive clothes put her hand on my shoulder. I turned from the skaters.

"Aren't you Helen? From New Orleans."

"Marlene! You look wonderful."

We shook hands formally. She was on her way to see her ed-
itor. She had become a sociologist and had written a book, but
she preferred not to divulge the subject. It was not quite finished. She *would* say it was about traditional male sexual hostil-
ity toward women. She understood much now that had been
cloaked in myth. She and Norman kept in touch. He was teaching art history in a small college in Nebraska. No, she had not
married again. Once was enough. There were more dignified
choices for a woman to make. We exchanged addresses. Since
we both lived in the city, she said, we ought to have lunch and
discuss old times. She used the word *discuss* often.

A week later, I received a letter from her. She had realized at
once, she wrote, that I didn't really want to see her. She was extremely sensitive to nuances hidden from most people. I had always been standoffish. How well she remembered that! Her
tone was accusatory and resentful, and I remembered something about her, too, that inflamed self-regard, how she had always been on the lookout for insult, a vigilance that exuded the
poison it fed upon.

Nina and I wrote for a number of years. But the exchange of
letters grew less and less frequent. She had eventually put herself through college. She had become a marine biologist and
married a fellow student, with whom she had two children.

Len went to law school on the GI Bill and with some further financial help from his parents. His choice of a profession
helped to soften their attitude toward our marriage and rec-
oncile them to a gentile daughter-in-law.

When we moved from Chicago to New York, I lost one box that had held the perfumed initialed handkerchiefs Rose Mayer always gave me for my birthdays, along with most of my personal correspondence.

But I had kept one letter from Nina in a small leather portfolio, along with personal papers, my teaching certificate for elementary grades, social security card, and other things of that nature.

The letter had been written a year or so after the end of the war, before Nina had begun to go to school. She had gone to France. She had wanted to see where her mother had lived in Paris, and then in a village in southern France called Giens. She had also visited some of the places Claude had told her about, the cemetery of Père-Lachaise and Marcel Proust's grave, the city of Blois, Chartres, and Chateaubriand's home in Combourg. From time to time, I reread the letter, and Nina's presence would steal over me like the fragrance from Gerald's wild garden.

> Claude had described it all to me with such liveliness and
> feeling [she wrote]. And it was as if he was with me when I
> went to those places, especially Combourg. It was immensely
> grand. You approach the chateau through a beautiful silent
> park. Claude told me that when Chateaubriand was a little
> boy and he misbehaved, he was made to sleep in a room
> in one of the turrets of the battlements. I went up a narrow
> stone stairway and walked along the battlements. I'm afraid
> of high places but I had to go on. I climbed a short flight of
> steps to a turret and opened the door to a room. It was
> not larger than your room in New Orleans. There was a high

bureau, a small bed, a chair, everything covered with thick dustcloths. It was late in the day. The light was cool and bright. I knew the custodian was waiting impatiently for me to come back down so she could call it a day.

I imagined that little boy walking to the room at night, perhaps wearing his nightshirt, frightened. I thought of Claude tracing his steps, and my tracing Claude's steps. I thought of the war and the millions who perished, and I recalled something Claude quoted: "Those who cannot remember the past are condemned to repeat it."

But, oh, Helen! Also those who remember repeat the past! And I thought of Lulu's death and Gerald's. And Claude dead beneath the oaks.

Are you still falling in love with people? Helen, don't forget me!

Part Two

CHAPTER

TWELVE

The nursing home where my mother died on April 3, 1967, two days before what would have been her seventy-third birthday, was on the west side of the Hudson River, a few miles north of Newburgh. The building was constructed of massive sandstone blocks; the windows were broad and deep-set, and there was a porte cochere where cars and ambulances paused to discharge elderly people in various stages of moribundity. Long benches were placed about the grounds beneath the old maple trees, but few of the patients were able to make use of them.

The owner of the nursing home was a nurse, Mona Gerow. She had been the "stout girl" Mother had hired to help her run the cabin business the year I went to New Orleans. During the months of Mother's suffering, Mona had been a great comfort to her. At the beginning of the long journey of cancer through my mother's body, I was abashed in Mona's presence. She was kind and downright with me but hurried in the conversations we had. I might have been an importunate but distant relative. Her business was pain and death. She was stern and efficient, but forgiving of the poor body's helplessness.

In the first months of her illness, my mother lived at home, but as the cancer gained more of her body's territory, she spent more time at the nursing home. I telephoned her regularly and went to visit her on most weekends. I taught the fourth grade in a private school in the city. The school did not use substitute teachers, and when there were emergencies and I had to see Mother during the week, my colleagues were burdened with my class. Their irritation at the extra work was tempered with sympathy. As time wore on, their sympathy weakened. I became a commuter between our apartment on West 113th Street and the nursing home. Whether I took the dusty train to Poughkeepsie or the bus to Newburgh, it was easier than driving. Sometimes I could doze for an hour.

In the middle of March, I covered the furniture with old sheets and locked the door, and Mother went to Mona and the nursing home for the last time. I went north ever more often. Len came when he could spare the time from a case he was involved with. He was defending a student who had been one of a group that seized control of the city university in New York to protest against the war in Vietnam, and who had also burned his draft card. Lydia went with me to see Mother twice but complained about having to take time away from her work for an organization called Women Strike for Peace.

A few days before Mother was taken by ambulance to the home, she wrote me a letter. Her handwriting was still strong and clear. The letter read:

Helen Dearest. We do not grow old in our secret selves. I thought I would become wise. I am not—though I've tried to study wisdom. I wanted to be wise about you, about the way you feel about me. Your last visit set me thinking. I saw that you were trying to be cheerful.

It's easy to forget that other people notice what you're trying to do to them with words and attitudes. I know how you hated it when you were a girl. I mean the way I always tried to look on the bright side. And you still do, Helen. Though you are kinder now. Getting older can make a person kinder, though not always. Of course you couldn't have known what the cost was. I was on the point of dying—not the way I am now—of giving up is what I suppose I mean. Lincoln had left me. It broke my heart. And it hurt my pride. But I needn't tell you about pride or vanity because you know all about those wicked things. Don't you, Helen?

I recollect your saying to me when Lydia was so sick with measles that I was not, for God's sake, to try to put a good face on it. I can still see how angry you looked. "My daughter is sick!" you yelled, as though I was trying to say different. I admit my way is not the best way by far.

But what you can't seem to forgive me for, Helen, is that it's the only way I know. During the years you were growing up (Helen, I can hardly bear to write this down but I must because my time is nearly gone and I want you to know this) I longed for Lincoln's arms around me the way a sinner longs for forgiveness. It made me insane some nights. I felt unmeasured. I felt I was turning into water and flowing senselessly hither and yon. I can't say more than that. I hope you never have to feel that way, though I think now that as terrible as it was, it is an ordinary desolation.

Well, I *am* dying now. It's not so bad inside, I'd guess, as watching it from outside like you are. I want to say I've loved and admired you. I never got over the surprise of having a pretty and very smart daughter. And I have had *lots* of good luck. The last months with your Aunt Lulu were awful! She was so domineering and so helpless. But we had wonderful moments. Once I got her two cigarettes, though she wasn't supposed to have them—but I knew it wouldn't matter by then—doctors can be so silly! And I made us a shaker of martinis—they were pretty weak. And we looked at pictures of ourselves when we were beautiful and men desired us, and we laughed so! It was a time when I looked into her eyes and really knew her. You wouldn't have recognized her by then, poor soul! Her hair had turned a rusty dead color, what there was left of it.

Oh, Helen! Forgive me myself! There isn't anything more. With all my love.

The letter was like a razor cutting me, silently, ever deeper. I read it frequently and carried it with me wherever I went. I showed it to no one. My heart sank below shame, to some dull gray place that I knew must be purgatory. From my apartment window, I looked at the river, at the snow clouds above the Palisades. I wept at the insufficiency of my understanding. I wept because I could not forgive my mother herself except with words in my head, while my heart, like a religious zealot, continued to read over the list of her heresies.

When I went to visit her the next time, she raised herself up from the pillow. "Did you get it?" she asked. Mona had just carried in a vase with the chrysanthemums I'd brought and put it on the windowsill. She patted my shoulder as she left. My mother's eyes followed her.

"Yes, I got it, Mother."

Her face was damp with sweat. She had been given morphine a few minutes earlier, and her words had begun to slur.

"I understood what you said, Mother." I had trouble swallowing; my mouth was dry. I was too hot in my heavy sweater in the overwarm room. I looked out the window at the limbs of a blue spruce.

"I'm sorry for the way I am, too," I managed to say.

"Oh, you're perfect," she said drowsily, smiling. "Your father was perfect, too. You take after him." She opened her eyes very wide then, and she winked at me. Her lids closed, and soon she slept.

The morning of the day she died, her face had utterly changed. Her small nose was like a knife because the flesh of her cheeks had withered so. Her eyes were sunken, dark.

"They stole the wood of the cabins," she muttered. "The place has gone to rack and ruin. We'll have to do something. I hated selling that fence that went around the course. Do you remember the horses cantering and galloping, and Lincoln with his stopwatch watching them? So tall and thin and elegant! Is Lydia all right? I hope she isn't in danger. The world is different. Everybody is so angry. Do you think people always have been angry, Helen, darling? And I didn't notice?"

I sat with her for several hours. Every so often I went outside and breathed in the cold air. "She's going," Mona said. "Dear sweet thing." There were tears in her eyes. "She encouraged me to study nursing, you know. I owe this place, everything, to her."

Toward dusk I had a sandwich in the nursing home kitchen. During the few minutes I was there, Mother died.

The funeral was held in the Congregational church she had belonged to for the last quarter of a century. She was buried next to Lulu in the small cemetery behind the church. A few hundred yards beyond it, I saw road-building machinery, and during the service I heard its growling and huge snarling as it excavated a new road. Next to the freshly turned earth of Mother's grave, the sunken ground above Lulu's bones looked like an ancient burial place.

The house had not gone to rack and ruin, although it had been neglected for years and everything about it needed work. One of the cabins was still standing. The outbuildings were gone and the course was an expanse of weeds and tall grass. The stable still stood. I looked at Len standing in front of the living room window.

"Are you glad to have the house?" I asked him.

"Have you ever seen these marvelous old photos, Mama?" Lydia called from the dining room.

"Of your Granny in plumes? Oh, yes."

"It's a nice house," Len said. He turned to look at me. "I liked her a lot," he said. I went to him and put my arms around him. "I'm glad for that," I said.

We planned to use the house in summer and weekends whenever we could. It was strange to think that now we were going to have a summer house. It had once been the only place I knew, substantial, seemingly eternal.

"What shall we do with the stable?"

"We'll think about it later," Len said.

"It's so musty and cheerless here. I should have tried to make it nicer for her."

"You were good and steady," he said. "You weren't supposed to come up here and wield a paintbrush."

"I don't know what I was supposed to do," I said miserably.

On a warm afternoon in early June that year, I ran into Nina Weir. There had been an emergency meeting at school. A sixth-grade student had brought a tiny cloth sack of marijuana to school and passed it around during art class. The teacher had spotted it. The boy insisted his father had given it to him. His younger brother was in my class. The principal and I were to have a meeting with both parents next week.

It was Friday, and I was going to drive up to the country after I did some errands. Len was in Washington and hoped to join me there late that night. Lydia was in Boston, looking for a job. I had the measurements for window shades for the house in my bag and was on my way to a store on Lexington Avenue where I could order them. I walked down Fifth Avenue as far as St. Patrick's Cathedral. The usual collection of ragged young people was milling around the steps. Even without signs bearing anti-war slogans, there was a feeling of an imminent demonstration.

A voice called my name. I looked up at the church. Just emerging from its doors was a woman about my age with short cropped hair, wearing eyeglasses. She was dressed in Liberty cotton and carried a large handbag shaped like a mailman's pouch. She ran down the steps, stepping over legs and arms. My heart leaped. We embraced. "Love, man," hooted a boy stretched out on a step, his head resting on a brown rucksack.

We walked for a moment, not speaking, our arms around each other's waists.

"Twenty-four years," I said, breaking the silence.

"No. Twenty-six. There's a place down the block we can get coffee. Do you have time?"

"Do I have time!"

We sat at a table the size of a tray, in two spindly chairs, and ordered iced coffee.

"We surely aren't the same," Nina said after a long pause during which we stared at each other intently.

"No. You've cut your hair."

"Oh, years ago! I'm not blonde anymore, just another brownish-haired person."

"When did you start wearing glasses?"

"That, too, years ago. My eyes were never strong. My daughter Erica began wearing them when she was seven. How is Lydia?"

"You remembered her name."

"She must have been around nine when we stopped writing. Why did we, do you think?"

"I don't know. Everything speeded up. There didn't seem time enough except for the daily things of life."

"What about Lydia?"

"She's pretty good. She's in Boston at the moment looking

for a job. Len made her take a secretarial course after she graduated from college. She went to Washington in 1963 and heard
Martin Luther King. She's been very political since then, very
serious."

"Erica is living in a commune outside Taos, New Mexico."

"Is that—all right?"

"There's nothing I can do about it."

"You have another child."

"My son, Claude."

The black waiter brought our glasses of iced coffee.

"He's in Canada. He went there to escape the draft. If he
comes home, he'll go to prison."

"So many people hate this war, Nina. When it's over, things
may change, and he'll be able to come home."

"Things only seem to change," she said.

"And your husband?"

"My husband is crippled and lost the sight in his left eye. He
went on a freedom march two years ago—in Alabama. He was
clubbed and beaten by a policeman and a local representative of
law and order and murder."

She stirred her coffee, then looked across at me.

"America kills," she said flatly.

"Oh, Nina! Don't!"

"He can walk, with difficulty. His leg was broken in three
places. He has what is called intractable pain."

The coffee was brackish and stale, and the tiny ice cubes had
already melted.

"But he'll get better? He might recover?"

"He may get a little better. You don't recover from being

beaten. You become different. The person you were saw life one way. You can't ever see it that way again."

I wondered if she had had some kind of religious conversion. "You were in St. Patrick's," I said, not quite making it a question.

"I looked inside. I thought it might remind me of Europe, of some French cathedral. It didn't. I had to pass among those infant drifters on the steps, smoking pot and exchanging the new inanities. But I saw something rather comical. There was a pretty girl sitting near the top of the steps. She was combing the hair in her armpit, a little puff of smoky hair, with a pink doll's comb—did you ever have one? The kind you got for a doll with real hair? She was holding her arm straight up and her head was bent and she was working so diligently with that tiny comb. Two boys were watching her and smiling with the most extraordinary smugness as though she were their peasant bride, standing in a doorway and carding wool." She laughed briefly.

Had I changed as much as she had? The short haircut didn't become her. She narrowed her eyes often, squinted, really. There were many wrinkles at the corners of her eyes and across her forehead, although her neck was unlined.

"But there have been good changes," I said.

"That's true," she said listlessly. She glanced at me. "You look so disappointed, Helen. How can I explain? There is a hard thing in my mind. I can't believe anything. What killed Claude and mutilated Gerald and crippled my husband, that brute thing, I see it everywhere. It's like Proteus. It can hide out in political attitudes that appear only benign. My grandfather was *chagrined* by the world. He thought evil came from simple willfulness. I suppose I ought to take up residence in a cave and eat locusts and cleanse myself of this awfulness inside me. I know it's wrong. I used to think, when I was a girl, that knowing you were wrong would make you change."

"You hated the way things were for black people," I said. "You used to think about everything. I always loved that, though it drove me wild sometimes, the way you didn't let things go by, the way you wondered and speculated. I swallowed anything."

She looked away from me, out the window at the people walking by. I didn't want to lose her attention. I sensed that I would if I continued to remind her of the way she had been.

"Do you live in New York?"

"We live in Bath, Maine. It makes it easier to get to Canada and see Claude. I teach biology in a high school. John's family helps us out. We have trouble with some of our neighbors because they know that Claude skipped the country. When John limps down the street with his cane, wearing his eyepatch, I expect there are patriots who feel he had it coming to him."

"You're so bitter," I exclaimed.

"Yes. I'm bitter," she said evenly. "I'm eaten up with it. I haven't been able to protect a single person I've loved. I know what people feel—the horror, the powerlessness—when they're forced to watch others being tortured."

"You named your son Claude."

She reached between the glasses of coffee and gripped my hand. It was mid-afternoon and there were only two customers in the place besides ourselves. For a moment I thought she would burst into tears. She only shook her head several times slowly. Then she said, "It was an added happiness when he was little, and I called him to me. Claude! Claude! Helen, do you remember him?"

"I remember everything. I remember you."

"He knew what to do about much that was difficult. But not *that* part of his life. It was why he understood me so well. I was floating—oh, I could take care of myself, find a job, a place to live, but I was just being carried along. His voice would come out of the garden at night. 'Are you there, Nina? Shall we take a walk? Listen to jazz?' And when I had to get away from Lulu— he said I could stay as long as I needed to, with him. I didn't know anything. He taught me how much there was to know."

"But . . . isn't there anything in your life now?"

"There's a good deal," she said, smiling as if she knew what I was trying to get out of her. "I like to teach. I like my students and our little house. I love my wayward children and my battered husband. He's not a bit like me. My God. He's even serene. He says the cause was honorable. He's become a fine cook. He thinks he'll try to write a cookbook when he's able to concentrate better. Do you ever hear from Catherine?"

"We wrote for a couple of years. She married someone eventually and went to live in Seattle and had a child."

"You wrote me when Lulu died."

"My mother's dead, too. Last April."

"Helen, I have to go soon. I got away because there's a teachers' strike at my school. I needed a few days by myself. But I have to go to a rehabilitation center downtown where John spent some months and get some material for him. I'm flying back home this evening."

"Will you write me? Could we see each other again?"

"I hardly ever write letters except to the children," she said with a certain gentleness, letting me down easy.

I felt so mournful, I wanted to lay my head down on the little table.

"I haven't asked you about Len," she said.

"He's fine. He likes his work, mostly civil rights cases."

"I wonder what happened to David Hamilton," she said. She frowned. "He was rather awful. I used to wonder why Claude put up with him. I've come to think it's because when you belong to a beleaguered group, you don't dare make harsh judgments about the other people in it. You don't dare because it might weaken the castle wall and outside, the murderous hordes are waiting."

She had been leaning forward as she spoke. She sat up straight and her face seemed softer. I could nearly see her as she had been.

"That was quite a time we had down there in New Orleans," she said. "I didn't know how good it was then, did you? Yes. I think you did. You were so mad about everyone, Gerald and Catherine, and Claude, too, weren't you? And Len."

"And you," I said.

"I thought intensely of you a few years ago. Do you remember that movie we were on our way to see on the day we heard about Claude's death, and there was such a terrific downpour?"

"*Star Dust*, with Linda Darnell," I answered at once.

"Did you ever see it?"

"No. I never wanted to after that."

"Did you read in the papers about her? She went to visit a

former secretary, in Chicago, I think. And they had planned to watch that very movie she had been the star of. It was showing on television. A fire started, and Linda Darnell tried to save some other people who were there and she was fatally burned. Isn't that something?"

I paid for the coffee, which we had barely touched, and we went out to the street. It was a beautiful afternoon, not too hot, buoyant and blue.

"Does Len still have that wonderful hair?"

"It's all white now."

"And did you ever fall in love with other men?"

I laughed. "A few. For a while. How can one not?"

She hugged me very hard as we stood there outside the restaurant while the black waiter watched us from behind the glass, his hands clasped behind his back.

"Oh, Nina," I murmured into her hair. "I can't bear it! Time . . ."

"Yes you can," she said sharply, drawing away from me but keeping a grip on my wrists for a moment. "We're made to bear it."

I watched her walk down the block toward Sixth Avenue until she vanished from view.

The last cabin had been knocked down and the lumber piled beside the spot where it had stood. As my headlights swept the site, I saw a family of raccoons flowing past the lumber like a tiny ash-colored stream. The moon was full; the Taconic Parkway had been like a great pale river. Slowly, reluctantly, I had come to realize I was relieved that Nina and I had not exchanged addresses. And I had begun to feel happy.

The house was black in the moonlight. For me it held a kind of historical weight. It did not convey the lightness I associated with the words *summer house*.

We had cleared out nearly everything except for the Chinese lacquered chest. The walls were painted white and the old floors sanded. The kitchen was completely redone. We hadn't bought much furniture, some wicker for the living room, a couple of tables and a standing lamp. Len's mother had sent us three Oriental rugs—small, intricately patterned and beautiful—which transformed the character of the room more than any changes we had made. Next week, I would have to order window shades at the store I'd been heading toward when I met Nina. There was considerable traffic on weekends, and people often halted their cars and stared at us without a trace of self-consciousness.

I turned on lights, including the porch light in case Len was able to make the last train from the city. I made myself a drink. It was strange to be throwing down whiskey and water in the new kitchen all by myself. It was after midnight. I was a little less happy now, unsettled, thinking about being fifty years old. Claude had been thirty-four when he died. I lifted my glass, to Lydia, to Len, to my life. I felt a tremor of fear, recalling Claude's god of nightmares who had failed him.

I glimpsed the dining room through the kitchen door. It was to be Len's study, but it was empty now. I had thrown away my father's ledger books, and all the trophies except one that Lydia had liked, a silver horse mounted on a marble base.

The whiskey tasted very good for once, and I made myself another drink and went to the living room and sat down in a wicker chair.

I must have dozed for a few moments. I awoke to the sound of a car idling on the road. In an instant, I was transported back to the times my father would be driven home from the train in a taxi, and I would hear his footsteps on the porch and come downstairs in my nightgown to greet him.

I got up and ran to the door and opened it. Len said, "Lord, I could die from tiredness." He came in and put down his brief-case. We rested our faces against each other the way I had seen horses do.

"I'm glad you made it."

"I nearly didn't. I was tempted to stay at the apartment and come up in the morning. Oh, it smells good here. The air is so fresh. I can smell cut grass. Are you drinking?"

"Would you like some whiskey? Or a cup of tea?"

"I'll sit for a minute. Then I'd like to sleep for twenty-four hours. Washington was a wring-out." He sank down on the couch where I had been sitting.

"Did it go well?"

"It didn't go anywhere much, like the bumper-cars in an amusement park, everyone banging into everyone else. Suddenly the time will be up, mysteriously ended. There'll be a decision, and the case will either go on to another court or it will stop."

"You'll never guess who I ran into in front of St. Patrick's today."

"I give up."

"Nina. Do you remember? Nina Weir?"

He was loosening his necktie. His skin was slack around his mouth.

He flushed. "Nina," he repeated. He looked over at me with such an expression of anxiousness, of apprehension, I imagined he had felt a sudden violent pain, the precursor of a heart attack, or else some other illness. It was a look I had never seen, not when Lydia was ill, or I was, when I had read in his face only his intention to make life's strongest effort for our sakes. It was awful to see. He seemed to be dissolving in front of me.

"Len! Are you all right?"

He brought his hands to his lap and pressed them against his lower belly.

"Len?"

"I'm all right," he said almost inaudibly.

"You're overworked. Come to bed right away. I'm going to make you a cup of Ovaltine. You must sleep."

"I'm all right, I said," he muttered.

I went to him quickly and knelt and slipped my arms around him. He stiffened and pressed his body against the back of the couch so that my hands were jammed against the wicker. With difficulty, I pulled them away and rocked back on my heels and stood up. He had turned his head toward the window at an awkward angle, his hands now clutching his knees. The moonlight was as thin as gauze beyond the glass.

"Len?"

"Well, how was she?" His voice was hard and clear. I laughed, not knowing why. Some immense and formless doubt had crept into my mind. I felt a touch of dizziness.

"Why, she's——"

"I think I'll get a glass of water," he interrupted, getting to his feet and striding toward the kitchen.

"But let me get it!"

"No!"

I could hear how strongly the new faucet ran. I was alone in the room. How strange it looked to me at that moment; it was pretending to be a new room. What had been the name of my father's woman friend? I had opened the note from her standing right where I stood now.

Len returned. There were drops of water around his lips.

"There was something between you," I said. I hardly recognized my voice, it was so thin and high, with something mechanical about it, like a talking doll's.

He leaned against the frame of the door, his arms hanging loosely at his sides.

I repeated what I'd said. My words came out slowly and distinctly but as though, I thought fleetingly, I had wrenched my neck.

He was staring at me.

"Say something!"

"It was a long time ago."

A sound came from my throat, a word, a cry, I don't know what.

"I must go to bed," he said. "There's nothing to say. There's nothing to talk about. I've been abused for two days by a judge, by other lawyers, by my own client. I can't go on."

"But don't leave me with this! Please!"

"Let me go!" he cried out.

"How dare you be angry with me!"

Had he smiled? He was walking to the staircase. He grasped the banister.

"You were in love with her."

"I was in love with her," he repeated neutrally.

"Why did you marry me? Wait! Tell me only that!"

He went up two steps. "Because I wanted to marry you, and you wanted to marry me."

Memory came like an arrow. "You were alone with her that night I took Lulu home from the hospital and stayed with her."

"I was alone with her more than once," he said. He yawned hugely. He was midway up the stairs. A car drove past the house at great speed.

"I didn't know you could be so heartless, Len."

"I didn't know you could be so foolish, Helen. It's history. We were young. It came to nothing. You and I came to something."

"Oh, wait! Tell me. Did she love you?"

"In time she might have. I don't know."

He disappeared from view. I heard his footsteps above in our bedroom. We often quarreled but not violently, not beyond repair. We made peace easily. Was that because he had held our life close to the surface lest this secret of his be unearthed?

I felt an access of energy that had fury in it. I flew up the stairs and into our room.

"You can't sleep," I said coldly. "I won't let you."

He was standing near the bed, his trousers on the floor. His socks were frowzy and his shirttail was wrinkled.

He said nothing and went off to the bathroom, closing the door behind him. I waited for his return, feeling such resolve—I didn't know what about—and such strength, I was convinced I could lift him and hurl him through the window. It was stuffy in the room. I went to the window and opened it. A faint scent of roses came into the room. My mother had planted climbing roses beside a trellis years ago, and they still grew there. They had flourished but grown ragged and tangled from neglect. I was not fooled by them. There was no history. We were no more than motes of dust, drifting so briefly through a narrow ray of light that we could have no history. The moon had set.

He emerged from the bathroom and cast a worried look in my direction. It was the look of a person who fears he will not be in time to catch the delicious, voluptuous sleep that is about to overcome him. He fell upon the bed.

"No. No, no, no," I said. "Get up. Sit up, at least. What am I to think?"

He rested his arm across his face so that it covered his eyes.

"Yes, think," he muttered.

"You can't be so stupid, so *cruel*, as to imagine I can put all this away like an old letter, something I can forget in the next hour. Our whole life together—she's been in it! What has our life been?"

"Stop."

"Why didn't you lie?"

"I didn't do anything. You told me you'd met her. I didn't know what I was going to do, to feel. How could I have? Tell me what I said?"

"I asked you—"

"Yes. *You* asked. Why did you *have* to ask?"

"It's always been between us. It explains so much. I've been a fool!"

"It hasn't been between us. There's been you and me and then Lydia—our life together."

"You were lovers."

Having said that, I covered my face with my hands and wept. He turned out the light next to the bed. In the dark room, my sobs were very loud.

"Were you?" I shouted at him.

"Do you wish Nina had taken your place?" his voice came wearily from the bed. "You made her take it with your aunt. And Mona took your place with your mother. Perhaps it would please you to think I've been mooning over Nina all these years."

"My God! Yes! There was Lulu, too."

He said nothing.

"What a horror marriage is," I said into the darkness.

"Yes," I heard faintly from the bed. "It is."

I went out of the room and ran down the stairs and into the kitchen. I stared at the whiskey bottle on the counter. Then I recapped it and put it away.

I went out the door and around to the back of the house. The stable loomed hugely, blocking out its shape against the starred sky. A soft breeze stirred the leaves of the old maple trees and elms around the house, but the elms were diseased and would have to be cut down.

Vague sounds reached me; nocturnal animals going about their work. Stumbling now and then, I reached the wall of the stable. A dog yelped once in the distance. I leaned my forehead against the old boards. Inside, I imagined the shades of my family, Lulu, Mother, my father, my awful old grandfather, gathered together in one of the empty stalls, listening thoughtfully, perhaps with some amusement, to the sound of my trouble.

We had both loved Nina. Len had guarded his love for her in secret, like a jewel in a tomb. But he had been wrong. It was I who had had a substitute life. I had taken the place of my father with my mother. I had taken Nina's place with Len. I was innocent.

I ran back to the house, through the door and up the stairs, taking two at a time, and into our bedroom, where I turned on the light. He wasn't there. I cried out his name. I went from room to room until I found him on Lydia's narrow bed, cast across it like a log deposited by a flood.

I grabbed his ankles and pulled him to the floor, where he landed with a thud. He lay still, his head on his hands, which were pressed together as though in prayer.

"You shit! You false cold bastard!"

He began to cry. Tears ran across his nose and fell onto the floor. I knelt down beside him.

"She's dry as dust," I informed him. "She's white as chalk. She's soured. Your Nina has gone, gone . . . She hasn't weathered well. She has the most ordinary brown hair. Her life is dreadful. You wouldn't have recognized her."

He drew up his legs.

"Speak to me!"

"Your little virtues," he said in such a low voice I had to bend close to hear him. "When you come back from the post office after you've mailed Lydia something she's forgotten. Your complacency. Doing what you ought to do. Hating it. You feel so fine, so neat in your dutifulness—and all that shows is how much you hate it all."

I rocked back and fell on my rear end, my legs stretched out in front of me. We both cried for a few minutes like children who have been caught out in mischief and are being punished together, exiled and shamed.

I got up and went downstairs, back to the couch. I slept for a while. When I opened my eyes, the room was not completely dark.

Year after year, I had come home from school and dropped my books on the floor of this room and gone to the kitchen to find something to eat. Mother was sewing or supervising workmen or putting away groceries she had brought home from Poughkeepsie. I would change from my school clothes, put on my sneakers, and go to the stable. My life was mine there, my thoughts simple and clear and sharp.

Over the meadow, the light was pale, but at the horizon there was a line of flame, the sun returning. The people who had stayed in our cabins were scattered, some dead by now, all old.

I went upstairs to see Len. He had gone from Lydia's room, and he was in none of the other bedrooms. He had been yearning for sleep, yearning to get away from me. He had needed a safe, hidden place. I saw the narrow stairs that led up to the attic.

I had played there on rainy days. In the high heat of summer, it had been filled with wasps building their gray papery nests. We hadn't cleared it out yet. When we looked at it one Sunday

morning, at the trunks and boxes and broken sticks of furniture, the old frames and the hat rack upon which my father had
often hung his fedora when he came home, Len had said, "We
don't have to face everything at once. We'll clean this out later."

I went up slowly. In those long-ago days, I had not understood why Nina had tried to avoid Len, and had been so stiff
and silent with him. My breathless confidences to her! My dec-
larations of love for him! How she had listened so thoughtfully!
How I had admired her tranquillity in her own aloneness! Len
had been looking past me, at her.

But I was so tired. The frenzied energy of the night had gone.
A certain pleasure in the vile scenes that had taken place between us had gone, too. Now and then I felt a tremor go
through my legs and arms. The liquor I had swallowed lay like a
hard, indigestible substance in my stomach.

I only wanted to find him and look at him.

He was lying beneath a dormer window that was covered
with dust-laden spiders' webs. He had gathered some old lace
curtains and made a nest for himself and he was sleeping. I recalled when Mother had bought those curtains. It was soon after my father had left. He had hated lace curtains, she had told
me.

I took off my shoes and tiptoed to him and sat down beside
him. For a while, I stared at the dormer window and considered the thickness of the webs, the way they softened the blue
light that was growing stronger every moment. There was a
powerful stale smell of old things. Mice lived among the trunks
and boxes and fed on discarded clothes and rags. We had heard
them at night.

Slowly, I lowered my gaze. There were dark circles beneath Len's eyes. A stubble of beard covered his chin and jaw, and there was a thin line of it just above his narrow upper lip. His shirt was open. The base of his neck was intensely white. I looked down at his bare feet. He was not luxury-loving, but he had always bought good shoes for himself when we could afford them, and his feet were nearly unmarked. For years, he had had trouble with a fungus he had gotten on an island in the South Pacific during the war. Often, he had been in such pain, he could hardly walk. When he went to his law classes, he sometimes wore shoes with so many holes he had cut in them, they looked as if they'd been gnawed by an animal. A delicate blue vein ran across each of his arches.

Suddenly, I could not hear him breathing. I thought, I've killed him, murdered him with hatred.

Then his eyelids trembled. He was dreaming. Was it a bad dream? A foot above him, I passed my hand over him, from the top of his head to his feet. I did not know why I had done that. I could hardly think. I had begun to feel sleepy.

His hair was still thick but white now. Nina had once said it looked like the breast feathers of a bird.

I remembered as I strained to keep my eyes open, when I had first seen him, how I had entered the ballroom and felt the darkness of the ceiling above before I had looked up at it. He had been standing at the foot of Aunt Lulu's bed.

I remembered how I had looked at him and wanted him.

I rested my head on my knees and sat there by him for a long time until he awoke.

Design by David Bullen
Typeset in Mergenthaler Perpetua
by Wilsted & Taylor
Printed by Arcata Graphics/Fairfield
on acid-free paper